1080 Kiss

1080 Kiss

Angela Steed

Black Lyon Publishing, LLC

1080 KISS

Our books may be ordered through your local bookstore or by visiting:

www.BlackLyonPublishing.com

Black Lyon Publishing, LLC
PO Box 567
Baker City, OR 97814

This is a work of fiction. All of the characters, names, events, organizations and conversations in this novel are either the products of the author's vivid imagination or are used in a fictitious way for the purposes of this story.

Cover Legs: Kerry A. Jones

ISBN-10: 0-9793252-5-0
ISBN-13: 978-0-9793252-5-0
Library of Congress Control Number: 2007934898

Written, published and printed in the United States of America.

To my family.

Chapter 1

Morgan Price finished off her morning coffee on the patio of her New York City house in her favorite white rocking chair.

The sun shone marvelously in the chalky blue sky as the birds chirped loudly in the backyard by the water fountain she had found at a local flea market the previous weekend. As she rose to her feet, she wondered what the day had in store for her.

She walked into the house, locking the French patio doors behind her with a sigh. The aroma of coffee filled her senses and she wished she could have another cup, but she was going to be late if she didn't get ready now. The meeting with her new client was in two hours.

Black slacks and a white silk buttoned blouse lay on her bed. She remembered rummaging through her closet the night before for her business attire. It was an odd feeling, like starting her career over completely. Wondering if the past three years had really happened, she had found the proof packed inside her old briefcase.

Papers with his name on them rushed memories back to her like it had happened yesterday. Most of them had been notes, telling her he couldn't make it to a photo shoot, or he was running late for a live interview on a national morning news segment.

She had shredded everything she found. It was time to start new. Fresh without consequence she had told herself while staring at the long strands of papers in the garbage can.

She noticed the blond highlights in her long brunette hair had faded. They were there a year ago, in fashionable strands of gold gleaming in the sunlight. He had always told her how much he loved them. It had been part of his seduction the night before she quit.

Morgan shook her head disappointingly, holding back the tears welling in her eyes. Sam Triton. How could she have been in love with him?

As his manager, there were rules she had set before she even took him in as a client. They were rules set by herself, and were mandatory depicted in the business ethics manual she had written for her company.

"There will be absolutely no personal relationships with clients."

Voicing them specifically to him every single night was tiring, and as his career progressed, it became harder to resist him. After all, he had become a famous rock star by the time she was finished with him.

It took two years to get him from amateur to superstardom. With his hauntingly beautiful deep voice, rock solid body that glistened pale with sweat, and below-the-shoulder black hair, he was the epitome of tall, dark and handsome.

Morgan scolded her reflection in the mirror for thinking about him. Taking off her bathrobe to slip into her slacks and shirt, she swallowed salty tears remembering that last night with him. If only she hadn't given in, she'd be with him right now. She wouldn't have wasted an entire year sulking in depression.

It wasn't really her fault. It was his for pressuring her too hard. He didn't have to pass up all the gorgeous half-naked women waiting for him after the concert and woo her while she tried to talk to him about his interview with a popular heavy metal magazine the next day. He didn't have to kiss her with his luscious lips making her completely melt like a block of ice on a scorching hot day.

It had all been a load of crap.

Every last tender word he'd said to her was a lie. Most likely they'd been lines he told all the other women he'd slept with, and there were many. She had wanted desperately to believe him. He was always so attentive towards her. Like a prince to a princess he had lavished her with gifts—expensive ones.

He loved giving her jewelry. She remembered the words he sang when he placed the diamond tiara he bought for her on her head.

"Queen of Triton, leader of the band, I offer you riches so you will sleep with Sam."

"What a jerk," Morgan thought, snickering at the memory. She had to lock herself in her room that sleepless night, indulging in chocolate truffles with the tiara on her head watching infomercials about skin care cream and rotisseries. With all the sleepless nights she had gone through with him, she had seen so many products that she could double as a salesperson for each of them.

Taking one last look in the mirror on the wall of her bedroom, Morgan was satisfied. In the year of lazing around the house, she was glad her figure hadn't been tarnished into a round behind and a plump stomach.

Of course, her friend and business partner Sally had made sure of that by forcing her to go to the gym with her at least once a week. And it was because of her she was finally going back to work.

"If you can't do this, I'll understand." Sally had told Morgan over the phone the week before. "But you can't dwell on what happened with Sam forever. Stop hiding in your self pity and get over it."

Morgan chuckled at the thought. Sally was persistent, strong willed and an all-around sweet woman. That she put up with Morgan taking off an entire year in the first place was enough to show that.

She tucked in her shirt as she made her way to the garage smiling at the thought of how wonderful it was going to be to see her again at the office. It would be an exciting adventure as it had always been in the past five years they had worked together.

She frowned as she started her car and pulled it out of the

driveway. She was diving into another world of countless opportunities. She only hoped the new client would understand and respect her decision to keep to business—business without all the personal attachments.

"The new Morgan," she thought aloud as she drove down the highway towards the city. "The improved business-conscious woman who does not mix business with personal no matter how hard the client tries."

Finding a place to park in the garage was easy. Between two tall buildings, a busy one-way street and a subway outlet, the high rise New York City office was like it had been in the past.

The noise factor was still there. She loved the familiar sounds of honking horns, shouting people and sharp whistles for the nearest taxi cab.

"Music to my ears," Morgan whispered as she walked through the revolving doors and around to the inside of the lobby.

Her heeled shoes echoed through the room as she walked across the gray marble floor towards the elevator. People waited with smug faces, watching the numbers flash above the door with an occasional sigh.

She stood with a bright smile, looking forward to seeing all the people she hadn't talked to or seen for the past year. She kind of felt bad for not checking in at least once in a while, but she was going to make up for the lost time.

When the elevator opened to a large familiar room, she smiled in delight. All the familiar faces, and new ones, stood in front of her greeting her with happy glances. It had been too long.

"Welcome back," they all said in unison followed by hugs, balloons and incoherent joyful mumbles as one by one they went back to their desks.

"It's about time." Sally grinned, taking her by the arm. She led her down the aisle of desks to her old office.

Morgan took everything in as she sat down in her chair. Nothing had changed. From her large cherry stained desk right down to the distant view of the Hudson River out the large walled window. It was like returning home.

Sally noticed the glimmer in Morgan's eyes and sighed. "It's so good to have you back. I've got to tell you though. I'm a little concerned if you're ready for all of this again."

Morgan hesitated as she watched a large tug near the mouth of the river. "I've missed you Sally." She turned back to face her, rocking in the black leather chair.

Sally's face softened. "I've missed you too."

Sally was so prim and proper. She was a late bloomer in college at the age of twenty-seven, but had already started a small PR firm in downtown New York working with the lower end stars in B movies and drama theatricals.

After they met in their first year of college, they became best friends. With Morgan in her jeans and T-shirts, pulled back long hair and bubble gum and Sally in her business suits, skirts and silk blouses, who sat with a stern unflinching stare as their professor lectured every day, they had been described as an odd couple.

Morgan had always wondered if she even owned a pair of jeans, let alone grew her short, cut-over-the-ear black hair out past her petite shoulders. But it didn't matter for she loved her like a sister.

Sally introduced her into her business and together they created Henshaw Relations. The public relations firm sent her on a quest to find down-on-their-luck musicians and bring them to the brink of stardom by selling their talent to major record labels.

Morgan loved it. Not only did it bring in a great income, it gave her the rights to let loose once in awhile as she went on the occasional tour with the bands.

Morgan swiveled the chair slightly back and forth with a smile. "Don't worry Sally. I'll be fine."

Sally leaned back with her elbows on the arms of the chair. She held her hands together at the bottom of her lips with a raised brow. "You're still in love with him."

Morgan stopped swiveling and stared at her for a moment. "I may have loved him, but I was never in love with him. There's a difference."

Sally reached over and took her by the hand. "It's okay. It happens to the best of us. Sometimes it's hard keeping our business and personal lives separate, even for me."

Sally stood up and walked to the window with a half grin, peering down at the ant-like cars inching through the city streets. She looked as guilty as a thief getting caught in a jewel heist.

Morgan watched her intently. "You've always been the essence of the perfect business woman. I highly doubt you'd find yourself in the mess I just climbed out of."

"Remember Kurt, the client I've had since our last year in college?" Sally paced the window, folding her arms over her chest.

Morgan noticed her smile had grown into the biggest grin she had ever seen. "I remember. Kurt Lanham, the actor you represented during—what was that movie called?"

"Plush Heroes." Sally sat back down in the chair and gazed at the ceiling. "Worst movie I've ever seen." She laughed.

Morgan eyed her, puzzled at where she was going. "So what are you saying Sally? Are you breaking the company rules of business and personal relationships?"

"He asked me to marry him."

Morgan felt as though her jaw had dropped to the floor and she couldn't find her hand to pick it back up. "You're kidding?"

Sally nodded her head excitedly smiling. "I agreed to marry my client. Now tell me, how could I pass up the opportunity to marry the most incredible, handsome and just all around wonderful man I've ever met?"

Morgan stood up in bewilderment and hugged her. "I'm so happy it worked out for you. When's the wedding?"

"We haven't set a date yet." Sally said, noticing the sadness in Morgan's eyes. She cocked her head with a sympathetic glance. "I'm sorry. I didn't think about how you might take it."

"I'm fine, really I am. I just ..." Her words trailed as she glanced down at the desk, tapping her fingernails lightly on its cherry glazed finish.

"It's just that you fell in love with a rock star." Sally finished her sentence.

It made complete sense. She had been warned before she took

Sam on as a client that rock stars had a tendency to be ornery, pig-headed and downright gritty. If only he had been different than the cliché of stereotyped hype she would still be with him, maybe even announcing that they too were getting married.

The phone buzzed, startling her thoughts, and a sweet high pitched voice came through the speaker. "Sally, Morgan's client is waiting for her in conference room two."

"Oh Regina, it's so good to hear your voice again." Morgan grinned in delight that her personal secretary had survived an entire year with Sally.

Regina Mills, the cute petite woman with an enviable head of long curly blond hair squealed in excitement. A loud rustling noise came through the speaker and Morgan knew she was on her way in.

The door swung open. Regina ran into the room with her usual puckered nose grin and gave Morgan a welcoming hug.

Morgan exchanged glances with Sally for a moment, smiling. Her client was here and the nervousness began to rise.

"Are you ready?" Sally asked.

Morgan nodded. She was embarking on a new adventure she wasn't sure she was really ready for. There would be late nights wondering if the client was going to show up for his photo shoot for some music magazine. Sleeplessness would take over as she worried whether he was going to make it to an interview on an early morning show or not.

Radio and television stations would litter the waves with his music as new videos and hits were released. Dealing with some cocky, overconfident and testosterone-driven lead singer of a rock band was mandatory for the next contractual segment of her life. This was what she did best, but was also her worst nightmare about to be relived.

Morgan entered the room expecting to see a bunch of over-dressed, stuffy looking older men sitting with a greasy, long haired, half-asleep man. But much to her surprise, she found a casually dressed older couple with sweet smiling faces.

"Morgan Price, I presume." The older man stood up and held

out his hand.

Morgan took his hand and greeted him with a smile. "Yes sir."

The tall gray haired man sat down with a humble sigh. "Don't call me sir. It makes me feel old." His blue eyes stood out as bright as the sky in midday as he laughed with the woman beside him.

"We're only in our sixties you know." The woman stretched her lips into a smile.

Morgan gave out a short laugh, obliging that they were the cutest couple she had ever seen. "What can I help you with?"

"Forgive my husband's manners. I'm Emma Evans and this is Ed." Emma grinned, showing such a lovely smile that Morgan wondered if she had walked into the wrong conference room.

She eyed the backwards number two on the window beside the door. She began to wonder if someone was playing tricks on her, initiating her first day back to work.

"Sally told us you're the best in the business, and we really need your help." Emma nervously cleared her throat. "She also told us you deal with musicians. Is this true?"

Morgan nodded in agreement, mesmerized by them. Never in her career had she seen a musician's mother come in as an acting attorney.

"Our son isn't really a musician. He's more of a—" Emma's voice trailed as she looked to her husband to take over. And just like clockwork he did.

"He's into pro sports."

Morgan set down the pencil she had been using to write down notes. The only things she'd written down were their names and the words "pro sports" with multiple underlines.

"I'm sorry, but I don't work with athletes."

Morgan knew they were troubled. And although they seemed to be the nicest people she had ever met with before, there was no way she could accept a contract from them.

Ed sat up in his chair and leaned in to the table with his hands clasped together. "I realize you only deal with musicians, in which case our son, Vince, is not unlike what I've heard about them. He's gone through four managers in the past three months. And with his track record, nobody wants to take him on as a client."

He reached down to his briefcase between his feet and set it on the table. Pulling out a thick folder filled with papers, he eyed Morgan.

She gasped silently, hoping they hadn't seen her reaction. It was indeed as thick as the most unruly musician's.

"If you read these, you'll see we've kept everything he's done. From all the good things, to all the rotten things he's pulled—it's in here."

Emma's emerald green eyes glittered with tears. "It's been his goal to become an Olympic medalist since I can remember." She wiped a tear from her cheek as Ed put his arm around her.

"Mr. and Mrs. Evans, I don't know the first thing about sports, and honestly I have no desire to mesh into a sports-related company. I've got to admit, if I agreed to be his PRM, I don't know if I would be of any help at all."

They sat for a moment, taking in what Morgan had told them. She hoped they would just get up and leave, but didn't want them to be too terribly disappointed.

"Listen, I'll contact some people here in the city and see if I can find someone who will take on a sports figure. I'm sure there are many that would love to have him."

She stood up, but seeing the sad expressions in their eyes, her heart sank. *You're getting soft Morgan,* she thought to herself as she sat back down in her chair.

"We've contacted everyone we know." Emma wiped another tear from her eye. "Our son is well known for his over precarious attitude. He won't show for any of his appointments, including this one." Her face brightened a little with excitement. "But we figured someone like you who's dealt with the rebellious types might find a way to help."

Morgan was taken back. Her face grew stern as she felt the softening in her heart slowly harden. "Mr. and Mrs. Evans, it sounds to me like you need a manager for your son. I'm all for making sure his appearances are set up, but actually seeing that he has made it to them is another job altogether. If he's having problems showing up for events, well, maybe he doesn't really want it as badly as you think."

"Thank you for your time." Ed said as he stood up and helped Emma to her feet. "We were hoping you could help us out, but obviously we've come to the wrong place."

"I'm truly sorry." Morgan hated to see such sweet people turn sour, and felt for them. "I hope you find someone who suits your needs."

She watched as they left the room. Sally walked in with a grin. "Well, how did it go?"

Morgan shook her head in disappointment. "It didn't."

"What happened?" Sally asked with a puzzled glance.

"Their son is an athlete of some sort. I told them I'd help them find someone else, but they still insisted I'd be the best candidate." Morgan lowered her voice. "Supposedly he's some egotistical jerk nobody wants to recruit."

Sally didn't look the least bit sympathetic for her dilemma, and showed it in her pursed lips. "Morgan. It's been a year since you've worked. You went through a lot to become what you are now just to give up on something new."

"I didn't go through five years of college to get involved as someone's personal manager, Sally. You of all people should understand that."

"But Morgan," Sally continued to argue, "isn't that what happened to your last client? You worked hard to get Sam where he is today. He's living the good life because of you."

Morgan glared at her. "I don't want to be someone's manager again. It's too close and personal with the client. It just sets me up for more painful aggravation." Tears welled in her eyes.

Sally frowned. "I'm sorry. I don't mean to drudge up unwanted memories. But Morgan, you can't put a hold on your career. If you wait for the perfect client, you'll be waiting forever." She gave a slight smile. "Maybe a change into something completely new is what you need. Screw the musicians and go for the hot bod of an athlete."

Morgan watched Sally leave the room. She swore she saw a skip in her step as she disappeared from the doorway.

Glancing down at the table, she saw Ed had left the folder, purposely no doubt. Not knowing whether to run after him and give it back, or just break down and look at them, she tapped her fingertips with a sigh.

"Curious," she said aloud, glaring at the thick stack of papers that beckoned her.

Giving in to temptation, she pulled the folder over with a heaving sigh of defeat. His name was written in permanent bright blue letters on a white mailing label. She read it aloud.

"Vince Evans."

She knew Ed had planned on this. He'd seen the softness in her eyes and took advantage of it. She was such a pushover.

When she opened to the first page, she cringed as she read an excerpt from a New York City Police Department citation. It accused Vince of starting a bar fight. That wasn't an unusual thing for her to deal with.

Sometimes things like this were set up for publicity stunts anyway. It could be fixed to his advantage.

She read through more of his files. Between donations to charity, bar fights, sitting in jail and parties galore, he was completely tame.

From what his parents had told her, he sounded like a true troublemaker. But in reality, she gathered he was more kind hearted than what they gave him credit for.

She closed the folder, noticing a paper clip with a card attached. It was the Evans' business card with a number written on it in big black letters.

She imagined Emma's raspy laugh when she told her the news she was accepting their offer. And suddenly she couldn't wait to meet her new client.

"Celebrate with lunch?" Sally leaned in the doorway and asked with pep in her voice.

Morgan grinned slyly. "Are you psychic?"

Sally rolled her eyes in thought. "No, I just know you too well,

Morgan. You can never back down from a good dish."

•

Morgan lay on her stomach on her bed with a glass of red wine in one hand and a piece of paper from his file in the other. She laughed, dangling her feet in the air and choking slightly every time she read something new from his records.

Regina sat on the floor inspecting the shoes and clothes that were flying from the closet every other minute. About half drunk, the cute, curly blond-haired woman would giggle every time a new item fell in front of her.

"Your wardrobe is pathetic." Sally huffed as she rummaged through Morgan's closet tossing things she thought weren't suitable for anything but a day of gardening.

"You say that every time you come over." Morgan eyed the mess on the floor and returned to reading.

"I'm going to take you out shopping one of these days." Sally twisted her lips at all the New York Yankees shirts hanging in one section together. "I thought you weren't into sports?"

"You say that every time, too." Morgan mumbled about spitting the sip of wine out of her mouth at what she had just read. "Oh, listen to this one."

Sally pulled out a pair of black hiking boots and inspected them curiously. Sitting on the edge of the bed near Morgan, she began to try one on.

"This happened about five years ago. A nineteen-year-old girl sued Vince for child support. She confessed she was pregnant with Vince's baby and already had a one-year-old that was his. After four court dates over a period of five months, the judge ordered her to a doctor's examination in Vince's defense. On the last day of court, her appalled parents showed up and confessed the one-year-old was her sister and that she wasn't pregnant. And the diagnosis of the doctor's examination said she was still a virgin."

"Oh my God." Regina laughed. "That sounds like the Dumb Criminal segment they have on the radio in the mornings."

"That's just terrible." Sally groaned, inspecting the heavy boots on her feet as she walked around in them.

Morgan grinned at her. "They look good on you."

Sally puffed out her lips. "Maybe I should try on jeans."

"Definitely." Morgan laughed. "Those don't go with your skirt."

"You know—" Regina cocked her head with a sheepish grin. "Vince Evans is quite good looking."

"Oh, I meant to check out his photo." Morgan pulled herself off the bed. She tiptoed through the piled mess of clothes and shoes on the floor and went out into her living room to get her laptop.

Sally took off the boots and found a pair of jeans in the floor. As she put them on, Morgan walked back in with her laptop under her arm.

"Sally's in jeans, call the presses."

Regina hopped on the bed with Morgan and watched as she searched Vince's name in the web browser. "There." She pointed at the first search line.

"Snowboarder, Vince Evans, the official web site. That sounds official." Morgan tittered as she clicked on the link, ignoring Sally's groaning as she looked at herself in the mirror.

A web page popped up with a picture of a man dressed in a black snowsuit in the middle of an aerial stunt. She couldn't really tell what he looked like from the distance the shot was taken.

"Maybe there's another picture of him somewhere."

She searched another site and when the page loaded Morgan and Regina both gasped. There he was, a large hairy man grinning in all his sprawled out glory.

"That's not your Vince Evans." Regina laughed, tilting her head to the side.

"Oh, that's just not right." Morgan puckered her nose and quickly closed out of the perverted window. "Let's try another."

Clicking on another snowboarding topic, she found a forum where people talked about their favorite winter sports events. Morgan found a post about Vince, labeled God of Snow. Curious, she read it.

"This guy goes to every competition Vince has been in and swears the man is a god," she said aloud, holding her glass up when Regina offered to pour her another splash of wine from the bottle. "He left a link to his fan site."

She clicked and the page began to load—a large grayscale image of Vince that was taking forever. His hair was black, parted off center with bangs down in his long thick eyelashes.

Excitement rushed through Morgan. He was handsome so far, but she wasn't sure that was such a good thing.

"Look at his eyes." Sally said, watching intently as big beautiful eyes stared at the three gawking women.

"I told you he was gorgeous." Regina elbowed Morgan with a half grin.

"Great." She sighed. "That's just what I need, another cocky womanizing man to treat me with disrespect."

"You don't know that," Sally scolded. "He might be a sweetheart. He looks like it anyway."

"Whatever." Morgan laughed nervously, watching the rest of the picture load. His nose was slanted perfectly with a slight point to the tip. And his lips? *Damn,* Morgan thought. His lips were parted into the most remarkably handsome smile she'd ever seen.

"I thought he was going to be a teenager."

"He's twenty-nine." Regina beamed rolling off the bed dreamy like. "Aren't you going to be twenty-eight soon?"

"December twenty-fourth." Sally grinned.

"Don't remind me." Morgan sighed, closing the cover of her laptop with a grunt before the rest of him downloaded on the screen.

Chapter 2

Morgan arrived at the party in style. In a snug-fitting black dress that showed a tasteful amount of cleavage, she stepped out of the limousine with a genuine smile. Greeted by Emma's doorman, she let him take her silk shawl from her shoulders.

The party had already started without her, even though it was in honor of her accepting the contract—and to meet Vince for the first time. She looked forward to it, but hoped he wasn't some gorgeous drunken clam looking for a pearl to swallow.

As she stepped down into the living room, she noticed Emma out on the back patio waving at her to join her with the hordes of people standing around her. She grinned nervously and walked out the sliding glass door.

People stood with prominent stares around an Olympic-size swimming pool, eating *hors d'oeuvres* off napkins in one hand, and drinking champagne with the other. Morgan felt like she'd joined a New Year's Eve party, but without the chilled winter weather.

Emma greeted her with a light kiss on the cheek. "I'm so happy you made it."

Standing next to her was Ed, smiling ear to ear with a raised brow. "I was about to come get you," he said, handing her a glass filled with champagne.

"Thank you."

Emma glanced around at the crowd. "Where is he, Ed?"

"He's not here yet."

Already ducking out on his responsibilities, Morgan thought, trying not to crack the smile that was curving her lips. That was typical.

"Oh, don't worry dear. I'm sure he'll be here soon." Emma said with a quivering glance.

Morgan took in stares as she mingled with Ed and Emma. They talked about everything from their remodeling project on their countrified kitchen, to the lodge they owned in the mountains. It was where she was going to be staying for the next few months, so she curiously asked questions.

"How far is it from the city?" and "How long is the snow season?" She also wondered how cold it would be in September, but didn't ask for fear it might be too silly of a question.

"I've never been skiing," Morgan confessed and took another sip of champagne.

"You've never been skiing?" A voice startled her. "Of all the guests we have here, at least some have caught snow before."

Morgan turned to face him. He looked just like the picture, except now he had sideburns that ran down his chiseled five o'clock shadowed jaw to the bottom of a pierced ear.

Any woman would melt in front of his stern green eyes and beautiful white smile, but Morgan stood as unaffected as she could. She had to—otherwise he might find the slightest bit of weakness in her and use it to his advantage.

He took her hand into his and kissed her lightly on its back. "Vince Evans. And who is this beauty?"

Morgan couldn't help it. She blushed, pure and simple. The warmth on her cheeks was assuredly showing and she turned away from his glance.

"This is Morgan Price, your new manager," Emma blurted out, smiling heartily.

Vince dropped her hand as gently as he had picked it up. "Oh." It was all he could muster up to say at first, but his thoughts ran wild. "Nobody told me I was getting a new manager."

Morgan smiled. "It's nice to meet you."

An awkward moment passed. Ed and Emma sneaked off into

the house, leaving Morgan and her handsome new client alone to talk. She couldn't think of anything to say and was glad Vince broke the silence.

"My parents think they're invincible. They've been married for at least a hundred years and are still going strong." He picked up a nearby glass of champagne and downed it quickly. "Sometimes I believe it's true."

Morgan took a sip from her bubbling glass. "They seem happy."

"They also meddle in my life too much." He stared at her with piercing eyes. "So I guess you know my history by now. Something you should also know is I don't like people getting in my way."

Morgan didn't want to argue, but she knew it was in good practice to get everything straight from the start. "From what I've read, you seem to have trouble with authority."

He laughed and began to walk, pulling her gently by the elbow with him. He led her towards the back gate of the pool and out into a small, quaint courtyard lit with solar lights along a paved walkway.

"Most people I've dealt with have tried to control me. I'm not too keen on power-hungry fame and fortune treasure hunters."

He stopped just before a stone statue of an angel spilling water from an off-green vase into a light blue backlit pool. Surrounded by green shrubs and well-groomed tulips, his sullen eyes looked like emeralds.

He set his glass down on the stone bench beside the fountain and grabbed Morgan by the arms. "Usually by now they would be talking a mile a minute about what wonderful things they're going to do for me."

Her eyes grew wide. Peering over the top of his shoulder as he leaned his face in next to hers, she could tell he was going to kiss her. She had to stop him.

As he leaned in farther, she leaned back keeping her distance. "If you think you're going to get a kiss from me, you may as well stop now. It's not going to happen."

"I was just testing the waters." He chuckled, sliding his hands seductively down her arms, and then letting her go.

She lowered her brows. "The waters here are cold and will remain that way through our contract." She took a sip of champagne, hoping the flushed feeling she had would dissipate soon. Finishing her drink off with a forced grin, she coughed lightly when it slid down the wrong way. "Control is what I'm best at, but treasures are not what I seek."

Vince let out a belting laugh. "You people are all the same."

She watched him sit down on the bench and stretch his legs out in front of him. He leaned on his hand behind him, staring at her.

"Curious," Morgan whispered, walking around the fountain, trying to control her trembling hands.

"What's that?" he asked with a scowling smirk.

"I said *curious*," she answered from behind the pouring water. She hoped he didn't sense the fear in her. After all the clients she had, none had been as perceptive as he was, and so free with his words at the beginning of the relationship.

He was sly. She could sense that from the start. Undeniably charming, whimsical with words, yet completely ignorant of how or who she really was. He was what she liked to call "a typical musician."

"What are you curious about?" He stood up and walked coolly around the fountain, slowly closing in on her.

I have to get out of this, she thought quietly, walking around the fountain from his dawdling chase. His mind games had begun and she was tired of dealing with him already.

"Don't be afraid to tell me your thoughts. We have a lot of time to finish this race, two years to be exact. That's plenty of time for you to find out what's going on in my mind," he said in a gentlemanly manner.

Morgan stopped on the opposite side of him and stared back through the waterfall. "I'm curious how you can tell me, who you've never met until tonight, that you know how I think, what I'm after, and that I'm just like every other person in my position."

Vince pondered. She wondered what really went on in that handsome head of his. If she'd met him under other pretenses, she would definitely have let him kiss her.

"There you are." Emma's voice sounded like heaven to Morgan's ears. "I've been looking all over for you," she told Vince. "You have a visitor."

Vince didn't acknowledge Emma's interruption. Without taking his eyes off of Morgan, he walked toward her slowly.

"Vince." Emma's voice grew stern, and it finally got his attention.

"I'll be there in a moment, Mother," he said coldly.

Morgan walked towards Emma, hoping she could get away from him. But he caught her by the arm as Emma sauntered off towards the pool cursing under her breath.

"I'm not finished," Vince said, letting her arm drop. "Since they insisted on hiring you, I want to make our relationship clear."

She agreed with a nod and faced him fearlessly. "Let me talk first."

He sneered, but lightened his face when he saw her glare. "Sure. Ladies first."

"Our relationship is strictly professional. In no way will you make any advances on me like you've tried in the few minutes we've known each other. Secondly, when I make public appointments, you need to show up for them otherwise you could lose sponsorship to events, and that could be detrimental to your career. Lastly, if you follow my lead I promise your career will take off quickly."

She was pleased at how it all came out and hoped he was going to accept it. But when he laughed, she could hear the cynical tone in his voice.

"What's so funny?" She fought the urge to push him into the water fountain.

"You." He chuckled. "You really are like them."

She huffed, trying not to burst into an angry shout. "I am not."

He lowered his brow and curved his lips into a scowl. "You think all I'm after is fame, but I'm not. I love doing what I do. It's who I am and I don't feel I need anyone else's help, especially not some prissy woman like you." He returned the cocky half-grin to his face. "The only thing you're good for is finding your way out of my business."

Morgan watched him leave, shaking his head as if he'd been shamed. She wasn't sure what to do, and crying over some jerk like him telling her off wasn't going to happen—ever.

She sat down on the bench, empty glass in hand, feeling like a failure. To think, she had two full years with him, contracted and signed. With his parents' desperation, there would be no way to breach it. The thought made her want to cry. And suddenly, as if the very fountain itself had dripped into her eyes, tears began to fall.

Weeping silently into the palms of her hands, a light touch on her arm startled her into sobering up. Wiping her cheeks with the back of her hand, she glanced up into Emma's smiling face.

"Don't worry dear," Emma said, sitting next to her with an empathetic smile. "You'll get used to his stubbornness."

"I know." Morgan grinned. "I'm used to dealing with it. It's just—"

"Oh, you don't have to explain. You know, Vince is just like his father when I met him." She took Morgan by the hand. "I met Ed in the fifties. We were only kids then, teenagers with the moon on our ass and the sun in our eyes. Getting into trouble was the only thing we knew. Ed, he used to go to the weekly Sunday evening worship and moon people through the window." She laughed at her memory. "What a horrible thing to do to such good people."

"Sounds like you had a lot of fun together." Morgan laughed with a sniffle.

Emma nodded. "People do strange things when they're young and ignorant, but it doesn't mean they'll be like that forever. I mean, can you imagine Ed's big white butt hanging through the church windows now?"

Morgan laughed and felt a little better. The tears dried from her eyes and thankfully she hadn't needed a tissue.

"Give it time, my dear. He'll grow out of it." Emma stood up and helped her to her feet.

As they walked back to the party, Morgan felt reassured by the pep talk.

But as funny as Emma's story was, she worried whether she was really prepared to go through this again.

Chapter 3

Morgan paced the room, walking along the window in her office with a scowl. "I've called him four times already, Regina. Where the hell is he?"

Regina sat in the chair with a worried look. "He's an hour late. I don't think he's going to show up again."

Morgan puffed out a sigh. "You'd think after two weeks of setting up this same appointment I would get the hint." Grabbing her purse underneath the desk, she dug through it and found her car keys. "I'm going out to find him."

Regina walked with Morgan to the elevator. "I'll hang out here. If he shows, I'll give you a call."

"Thanks." Morgan smiled from the elevator before the doors closed.

Every day for the past two weeks she had called him numerous times to set up the consultation. Unsure if it was fear of seeing him, or the fact she was going to wring his neck for doing this to her, she had refrained from going out to find him.

"Jerk," she said aloud as she rode the elevator to the lobby. "He's not getting away with this." She took out her cell phone and dialed Emma's number. "I've resorted to telling his mom on him." She laughed with an irritated glance as the elevator doors opened.

It was an immediate forgiveness when she saw him. Dressed in a tight-fitting black T-shirt that showed off his well-built arms and chest, jeans that were filled out marvelously, and those bright green emerald eyes that stared at every curve of her body, Vince stepped inside the elevator beside her.

"Good morning," he said grinning at her mischievously.

Morgan still held her cell phone to her ear with her mouth agape. Trying to control her trembling lips, she stuffed her phone back inside her purse and straightened her thoughts.

"I've been trying to contact you for two weeks now." She frowned as she pushed the button to the office floor.

"I know."

"So what made you decide to show up all of the sudden?"

Vince chuckled. "I think I was tired of hearing ten messages a day asking me to come in so we can talk."

"Your professionalism is lacking," she growled. "At least try to make a legitimate excuse."

The elevator opened to the office floor and they both stepped out. Vince followed her to her office, making eyes at all the women gawking at him as he walked through.

"Regina, hold my calls." Morgan smiled as they passed.

"Yes, Ms. Price." Regina's eyes were wide, staring at the beautiful man walking by.

Morgan understood completely. She too felt the same way as all the other women in the room, wanting to stare at him. Too bad his personality didn't match his looks.

She shut the door to her office when he sauntered into the room. "Have a seat," she said as she sat down in her chair.

Curious, Vince walked to the window with a smile. "Nice view."

"So tell me, what are your goals for the future of your career?" she asked, getting right down to business.

Vince paced the window leisurely without taking his eyes away from the view of the river. "Near future or distant?"

"Let's start with near future," she answered, trying to keep her eyes on the back of his head rather than the way he filled his jeans out perfectly.

"One of my goals is to take you out to lunch." He grinned slyly.

Morgan swallowed hard. A lunch date with her client was perfectly harmless she thought. "I'll agree to go to lunch with you if you promise to answer your phone when I call."

He laughed. "Sure, I promise."

Morgan wasn't sure if he really meant it by the way he smiled. It wasn't a smile of defeat, but it was something she was just going to have to trust him with. That wasn't saying much.

"Okay, that's one accomplished. What are your others?" she asked, curious to hear the next.

He sat down in the chair, eyeing her with a raised brow. "Are you a psychologist?"

"No."

"Then why are you asking me these questions?"

Morgan sighed. "Curious, I guess."

"Curious about what?"

"I'm trying to understand how you lost your sponsorships." She leaned back in her chair. "Sometimes celebrities lose sight of why they do what they do. Typically when this happens, they tend to miss important occasions—interviews, photo shoots or whatever else they're involved in."

She swiveled nervously, feeling the tension thicken in the air as he stared at her. She wasn't sure how he would react, but she had to get through to him somehow.

"I'm just wondering if you might be, I don't know, burned out. Maybe you're tired of being the star on the mountain and would rather be the ship sailing on a calm sea."

Vince opened his mouth and Morgan was ready for him to blast her with profanity. She wanted it, at least then she'd understand his true intentions about his career. It was the same thing she'd said to Sam to straighten him out and had worked like a charm. But just as Vince opened his mouth, he shut back up and flashed an amused grin.

"I see what you're doing here, but it's not going to work." He stood up and walked around to her. Sitting on the desk in front of her, he picked up a pencil and stuck it over his ear. "Seeing that you're not going to give up like all the other managers I've had, I'll make you a deal."

Morgan's heart pounded in her chest as he leaned in close to her. She thought he was going to try and kiss her again, but he stopped just inches before her face.

Without a flinch or a breath, she gazed back into his eyes. "A deal?" she whispered with a quivering voice.

He nodded, lowering his eyes to her mouth, then back to her eyes. "If you can keep up with me for the next two months, that means going where I go and doing what I do without quitting or complaining, then you have my cooperation."

"Technically—" Morgan swallowed, pushing herself away from him. "I don't have to do anything of the sort. I don't like games Mr. Evans, and I'm not going to play yours."

He chuckled, shaking his head in amusement. "Suit yourself." He jumped off the desk and walked to the door. "It's not just my ass on the line here. Just think. If you fail, word might get around you're not as good as people think. That could put a hurt on clientele."

She felt like exploding into little fiery pieces. "How dare you make threats," she shouted, stomping towards him with a hand ready to slap him out of her office.

"Whoa, hold on there." He grabbed her by the shoulders and laughed at her outburst. "I wasn't making threats. Just think of it as a way to study why I am the way I am." He winked.

She gained control of her temper, hating the way he turned her from a steaming fireball into a softened pile of mush. She sighed.

"Fine. You call and I'll be there."

"Great." He let go of her shoulders. "Then meet me here tonight." He handed her a small piece of paper with writing on it.

"Joe's Bar?" Morgan puckered her nose. "Great. The bar scene."

"Your sarcasm is duly noted." He glanced at her white silk blouse and navy blue polyester skirt with a sigh. "Make sure you change into something less stiff before you come. And be there at six."

Morgan watched as all the women in the office melted when he passed. He may be the best looking man on the planet, but he was still a complete jerk. Of course, she thought as she slumped back down in her chair with her eyes closed, he knew how to play her game. And right now, she was losing.

•

Ten minutes until six o'clock and he wasn't there yet. As Morgan waited in the parking lot in the safety of her car, she wondered if he had set the whole thing up. He wasn't going to come, and she was fool enough to believe he would show.

Fifteen more minutes, and that was all she was going to give him. Not one second later, she thought, turning on the radio to keep the silence from driving her crazy. But as soon as she heard Sam's voice, she quickly switched it off.

"This is ridiculous." She scolded herself as she started the car. "He's not going to show."

With a huff, she shifted into gear just in time to hear a knock on the window. It was Vince, smiling at her.

She cursed under her breath for being startled. After one last glance at herself in the rear view mirror, she opened the door and stepped out.

"I'm willing to wager you thought I wasn't going to show." He chuckled as he closed the door for her.

"The thought crossed my mind." She wondered what he was eyeing on her shirt and followed his smirk. "What is it?"

"You're not quite dressed for this place." He twisted his lips to the side.

"You said casual." Morgan looked down at her plain gray T-shirt and light blue jeans over white sneakers.

"I'm going to have to take you shopping."

He took her by the hand and led her to the side of the building. Motorcycles lined the outer wall as if a biker gang had parked there. She stopped in her tracks when he walked up to a bright red and black street bike and stopped.

"I'm not getting on that thing," she stammered and refused the black helmet he held out for her.

"Yes, you are." He put the helmet on her head.

"I don't know," she said.

As he snapped the buckle under her chin, he saw the worry in her eyes. "You're a big baby." Seeing the glare overtake the worry in them, he knew she'd changed her mind despite his comment. "You're also a stubborn woman."

"And you're a big jerk." She watched him mount the bike and pat the seat behind him for her to join.

"Get on."

She hesitated briefly, but as she looked into his peering eyes from the opening in his helmet, she couldn't resist any longer. She hopped on the back not knowing where to put her hands as he started the engine.

"Haven't you ever been on a motorcycle before?" he shouted back at her.

"No."

He grabbed her hands and pulled them around his waist. "Hold on."

Her heart beat fast as they sped off down the road. Her hands trembled and she squeezed him tight, closing her eyes.

"You're going to squeeze the wind out of me," he shouted back at her and tapped on her hands as they stopped at a red light.

"Sorry." She loosened her grip, opening her eyes just as the light turned green. "Where are we going?"

"You'll see."

She was beginning to enjoy the ride although her hands still shook. A smile escaped her lips when she noticed they were leaving the city limits.

It had been a long time since she'd been away from the city. To get out and enjoy the open, late-August air rushing through her was a real treat. And after an hour and a half of riding, Morgan was so comfortable she felt like throwing her hands in the air as they flew down the highway.

It was an amazing sensation as they passed cows grazing in green pastures. It looked like something off one of the country magazines she'd seen at the store. She'd always thought it would be wonderful to have such a place. And at sunset, the countryside was more beautiful.

"We're almost there," Vince yelled back with a grin.

She held on tight again as they pulled off the highway and rode into a store parking lot. She was puzzled as they parked in front of a large building that looked more like a warehouse than a store.

"A sports outlet?" Morgan asked as she watched him dismount. "What are we doing here?"

Vince took his helmet off as she stood up and swayed a bit. "Dizzy?" He took her by the hand before she fell.

"A little bit, yeah." She laughed, planting her feet on the ground. "I'm okay."

He watched her intently as she leaned down and pulled the helmet off. She flipped her hair back and stumbled slightly, keeping her balance with his hand. Her hair fell down around her shoulders to the middle of her back, making him smile at her.

"What is it?" She tossed her hair back from her shoulder. "My hair's a mess and you're laughing at me."

"No." He locked the helmets in place.

"Yes, you are." She huffed and followed him into the store.

"Just come on. We have shopping to do." He took her by the hand and led her through the giant store.

She was awed by all the sports equipment. There were canoes hanging from the ceiling, bikes, skis, guns, fishing poles and just about anything that had to do with the outdoors.

It wasn't until they reached the clothing did he stop. "I'm not much of a shopper, so I'm just going to let you pick out whatever you want."

Morgan looked up into his face and realized he didn't have a clue where to take her. Not wanting to start a fight since he was being nice, she smiled graciously and began looking around.

Using Vince as a guide, she picked out a few outfits that would be suitable for a day in the snow. But since it was still hot outside, she stuck mostly to the summer items.

Most of the outfits came with a logo on the top left of the shirt, similar to what Vince was wearing. So she stuck to picking out various colors of the same kind of shirts, shorts and tennis skirts.

"I've got to say, this is the strangest thing I've ever encountered with a client. I'm used to overly expensive restaurants and fine jewelry." She found a navy blue windbreaker she really liked. "I mean, considering the people I've traveled with before, this kind of gift giving would be out of the question."

"Do you always show your appreciation like that?" Vince asked and took the clothes from her with a frown. He draped them over his arm and made his way to the checkout.

"I didn't mean to sound rude." She followed him.

"It came out that way." He watched as a blushing young woman started ringing up the clothes.

Seeing the girl's rose colored cheeks, Morgan wondered if any woman was able to resist him.

She put her helmet on and hopped on the seat behind Vince. She looked forward to the drive back, although it was almost dark. And soon she wasn't going to be able to see anything.

Vince hadn't said a word since the check-out, and she was beginning to think he really was angry with her. She tightened her grip around his waist and wished she hadn't said that.

It was completely dark by the time they reached Joe's Bar. The parking lot was full. As they parked on the side of the building, Morgan noticed other cars were blocking hers in.

"Damn." She pulled the helmet off and glanced around as if looking for the idiots that had parked there.

Vince let out a disappointed hiss. "Oh man, that's tough. Looks like you're going in with me for awhile." He grabbed her by the hand and started walking towards the entrance.

"Wait a second." She stopped, pulling her hand away. "I'm not going in there."

He turned around and chuckled. "Guess you should put your bags in the car. Come on."

Morgan pulled the keys from her purse and unlocked the car door. She was about to toss the bag in the back seat when Vince stopped her.

"Wait. You should change first." He hopped into the driver's seat. "Get in back and change into the blue outfit."

"What?" Morgan gasped as he closed the door grinning.

Morgan stood there briefly, glancing around to make sure nobody was nearby. She opened the passenger side door and crawled into the back seat, glaring.

He turned around and opened the bag. He pulled out the baby blue spandex tank top and white mini tennis skirt she'd picked out.

"That's for playing tennis." Morgan laughed when he handed her the clothes.

"Trust me. This is perfect for this place." He smiled.

"I'm not wearing that."

"Yes, you are."

"No, I'm not."

"Yes, you are."

She could tell he wasn't going to take no for an answer. "I'll put on the shirt, but I'm not wearing the skirt."

She grabbed the shirt from him with a sigh. "I can't believe I'm doing this." She pulled her T-shirt over her head.

Vince kept his eyes forward, trying desperately not to turn around. Glancing in the rear view mirror, he caught a glimpse of her pale skin. A grin escaped his lips.

"You should put the skirt on," he said just as she climbed over into the front seat.

"Do you want people to think I'm a nut? Because that's what I'd think if I saw—"

"Are you ready to go in?" he interrupted, watching her pull her hair up into a clip.

"I suppose," she said nervously.

She loved the way the tank top felt against her skin. The stretchy material was perfect for a warm summer night, although she wouldn't have worn it to a night club. But she had a feeling Joe's Bar was going to be a lot different than any other bar she'd been to.

Vince took her by the hand as they walked through the entrance into a large room filled with people. She was right. Everyone was dressed in sports clothing. From football jerseys, spandex shirts and—she laughed at the sight of it—tennis outfits.

Plasma televisions hung on the walls around the entire room with different sports channels on each one. The music wasn't loud, but that didn't seem to bother anyone.

As they walked towards the bar, a few people stopped Vince to say hello, including a woman dressed like she had just come from a beach in Hawaii. Her flower print bikini with a see-through silk skirt matched the purple flower in her hair.

"Oh no Vince, please tell me you're not getting married," she whined. Her voice sent chills up Morgan's spine. It was like a shrill high-pitched banshee's scream.

"No, Kathy, I'm not getting married." He kissed her on the cheek with a smile, sending the girl into a bubbly fit of giggles.

Morgan felt like she was going to be ill. Leaving Vince to the woman's story about her exciting trip to Hawaii, she headed toward the bar.

"Can I get a glass of red wine?" she asked the bartender.

He ogled her. "We don't carry wine here."

"No wine?" Morgan pulled herself up onto the bar stool. "I guess I'll have a diet cola then."

He softened his face and grinned. "How about I make you a nice mixed drink?"

"I can't stand the taste of liquor." She frowned.

"Let me make this for you on the house. If you don't like it, I'll go out and buy you a bottle of wine."

Before Morgan could argue, the man was already making the drink. She glanced down the bar and noticed there were several men grinning at her. It felt nice to be stared at, although a little disconcerting.

She looked at the drink the bartender set in front of her. A red concoction in a tall glass, which meant there was probably a lot of alcohol in it. He stared at her as he reached underneath the bar and pulled out a bright yellow straw. He added it to the drink, making it look exotic.

"Bottoms up."

She picked up the glass and hesitantly took a sip. It was surprisingly good. "What is this?" she asked him, taking another refreshing sip.

"Sex on the Beach," he replied with a grin. "You like it?"

Morgan nodded with a smile. "Thanks."

"There you are." Vince sat down on the stool beside her. "Hey Jim, how about a beer?"

"No problem, Vince."

Morgan could feel the liquor already. She hadn't meant to drink it fast, but she was never good with alcohol. It was either too much or none at all, but she decided to try to savor the next one.

"Don't drink too much or you'll miss out on the fun." He chuckled as she started sipping on a new glass.

"Miss out on what?" she asked curiously.

Vince pointed to the doorway on the back wall that led into a darkened room. "That room is what makes this bar so popular with the winter sports crowd. You'll see what I mean when they open it up at eleven-thirty."

It was eleven and Morgan couldn't wait to find out what made the place so special.

"How about doing a couple shots with me?"

"Okay." Morgan sipped the last of her second drink through the straw and set down the glass.

He ordered each of them a shot of tequila dressed with lemon and salt. She'd seen Sam do the same thing a few times but never joined him, especially after seeing the drunken outcome.

Unsure if it was because the whole day had been unusual for her or the fact she was already tipsy, she grabbed the shot and downed it fast. It burned her throat and made her eyes water.

"You're supposed to lick the salt first." Vince laughed, handing her a slice of lemon to suck on.

Morgan opened her mouth for him to stick the lemon on her burning tongue. The sour taste made her pucker.

"Want another?"

Morgan pulled the lemon from her mouth and sighed with a woozy grin. "Sure, why not?" she agreed as she watched him down his.

As Jim poured another shot, she pulled the clip from the back of her head and let her hair fall down around her shoulders to the middle of her back.

Morgan licked the salt from her hand and downed the shot just as a rather large man sat down on the stool beside her. She grabbed the lemon and sucked on it quickly, diminishing the burn on her tongue.

"I wish I was that lemon right now," the man said, grinning at her with wide bloodshot eyes.

Morgan set the lemon down on the counter ignoring his rude comment. The alcohol was working on her too much for her to get upset.

"A beautiful woman like you probably has a lot of experience. Why don't you come home with me and show me your skills?" The man pulled on his crotch.

Morgan turned away from him in disgust, hoping he would go away if she ignored him. Vince was talking to someone about a football game playing on one of the TVs.

The buzz that swam in her head made her feel uneasy. She was going to end up drunk if she didn't slow down, which would leave her car stranded while she took a cab home. But at this point, Morgan knew it was inevitable anyway. She was definitely not sober enough to drive.

She watched her feet woozily as she stood up to go to the restroom. Being careful not to fall, she tiptoed a few steps, but ran into the rather large man who had made the rude comment before. He stood almost an arm's length overtop of her making her eyes widen.

"Want to dance?" he asked grinning down at her.

Morgan looked up in awe and frowned. "No thanks."

"Sure you do." The man grabbed her wrist with a smile.

Morgan pulled her arm away trying to focus on where she was going. "Leave me alone."

He smelled of stale beer and body odor, and was completely smashed by the way he swayed. She couldn't imagine standing near him when he passed out—he would surely crush her with the mass of his body.

"Come on, baby. I'm a good dancer." He grabbed her wrist again, but this time it hurt as he pulled her towards the dance floor where nobody was dancing.

"Let go of me, you Neanderthal!" she cried out, jerking her arm back.

He suddenly stopped, making her run into him. She peered around his body and a smile popped across her face.

"Hey man, what's up?" Vince confronted the drunken man as he stood between him and the dance floor. "Why don't you leave her with me and go sleep it off somewhere?"

Morgan felt the man's grip loosen enough for her to free her arm. As she stumbled slightly behind Vince, the large man frowned. This was going to end up in a huge bar fight. She knew it was going to happen and it would be her fault.

"You really don't want to mess with me." The man held up his fists. "I was the heavy weight boxing champ five years in a row at my university."

"Come on, Vince. Just leave it alone." She took him by the hand and pulled at it, but he refused to go with her.

"No, this guy owes you an apology." Vince eyed the man, ready to plant his fist on his jaw if he made a move.

Morgan cringed as she compared their difference in height and weight. Vince wouldn't stand a chance against this guy, and would be signing a death warrant if he fought him.

"Come on. Let's just go back to the bar and have another drink." She stumbled again as she stepped away, but the huge man caught her by the wrist.

"The woman wants to go home with me." He pulled her hard over to him smashing her body into his.

"What is this guy, a caveman?" she whispered through clenched teeth, waiting for him to grab her by the hair and drag her away. But just as she thought that, Vince threw his fist against the man's jaw. She heard a loud crack and the man tumbled over to the floor, letting go of her arm.

Vince caught her around the waist and picked her up before she fell to the floor along with the man. He set her down behind him and turned to go another round with the man. Luckily, he was drunk enough to stay down on the ground until the bouncers came and dragged him outside.

"Damn it, Vince. You can't go around protecting every woman who gets into trouble."

She made her way to the bar where another round of shots waited. She downed hers fast as she sat down on the stool. Sadly, she was intoxicated enough she didn't need the lemon anymore.

Vince raised his brow when he sat down. "So you're telling me I should've let him force you into going home with him?"

"No, I'm just saying ... " She lost her train of thought and laughed drunkenly. "I don't know what I'm saying. Just don't start any more fights. I'm your boss and you have to listen to me."

"You're drunk." He chuckled and stretched out his sore hand.

Morgan noticed the lights were on in the back room and people made their way inside. She was curious. She'd imagined a bronco ride inside, but couldn't possibly see Vince riding it.

"I'll let someone else make a drunken fool out of themselves first." Vince laughed as Jim poured them another shot of tequila.

"I can't drink anymore." Morgan laughed, leaning against his arm. "If I do, I'm going to pass out and I'm having way too much fun to want that."

"Come on, one more and then we'll both quit."

"Are you drunk, too?" She leaned in closer wanting to kiss him, yet still hanging on to that last shred of will power she had.

"Unlike you, I can handle my drink."

"Oh." She sat back up in her stool trying not to fall off the other side. "I guess you're right. Are you going to ride a bronco?"

He laughed. "No, not quite." He helped her to her feet and grabbed her shoulders to steady her swaying. "Come on, I'll show you."

She held onto his arm as they walked into the room. It was

much colder than the room with the bar. And when everyone saw Vince walk in, they started shouting his name.

He led Morgan through the cheering crowd of people and across a small wooden bridge. She felt like she was walking him to the concert stage for his performance with all the outstretched hands. That was something she'd never done before with Sam, but had seen it on many occasions.

When they stopped along a small wall in the center of the room, he turned her around to see what all the hype was. A gasp escaped her lips. A snow maker was spitting out snow on a small halfpipe all the way around the room. There were curved ramps and tunnels along the outer wall just waiting for him to ride.

From the outside, the building didn't look like it would be big enough, let alone the ceiling high enough for anyone to catch air. But here it was—the strangest and most unique thing she'd ever seen inside a bar.

"Amazing," she said as Vince leaned her against the wall near a rack of snowboards.

"Try not to fall." He steadied her before he picked out a black board from the selection. "I'll be right back."

Morgan watched him climb to the top of the ramp and take off immediately. He slid down the hill and back up the other side, gaining speed. He shifted the board back and forth as he caught air off the first ramp.

The crowd cheered. She enjoyed hearing it as he stood on his hand at the top of the ramp and then slid back down towards the tunnels.

She wished she wasn't drunk. She wanted to enjoy it just as much as everyone else was, but her vision was so blurred she could barely see him. She slid down the wall and sat down on the floor, trying to control the spinning of the room. Cursing at herself for drinking too much before the party even started, she closed her eyes.

It seemed like she was out for only moments until she felt strong hands on her shoulders pulling her up. Groaning, she opened her eyes and realized someone was walking with her outside the bar.

She smiled when she saw him.

"You're wasted." He laughed as they made their way across the street to a hotel.

"Vince, my beautiful green-eyed guardian. You're taking care of me." She put her arm around his waist and laughed with a hiccup.

"Wait here and I'll get us a room." He sat her down on a couch in the lobby and watched her fall over slightly.

She tried not to pass out again. He was getting her a room at the hotel across the street knowing she was too drunk to drive home. That was a good thing.

She opened her eyes and smiled at him as he picked her up off the couch.

"You're such a sweet man." She leaned her head against his shoulder. "I love you." She sighed. "You made me ride your motorcycle, which was scary and wonderful. And you bought me clothes."

When they made it to the room, he laid her down on the bed and helped her take her shoes off.

"I'll sleep on the recliner." He glanced down at her, knowing it wouldn't make a difference what he said to her right now. She wasn't going to remember a thing when she woke up.

Morgan clumsily sat up and took off her tank and jeans. "Don't be ridiculous." She moved under the covers and opened the other side for him. "It's okay. I trust you."

Vince sighed. "Alright, but don't scream when you wake up and find me in bed with you."

"Okay. I promise."

She watched as he stripped down to his boxers. The creases on his abdomen were chiseled to perfection. His rounded pecks seemed to cry out for her touch. And she desperately wanted to touch them.

As soon as he got into the bed, she leaned on his chest and closed her eyes. The warmth of his body felt wonderful on her cool skin.

"I had a really good time tonight," she said, raising her eyes to meet his.

She leaned down to kiss him lightly on the lips, but missed and buried her face in the pillow. The alcohol had finally won.

"Morgan." Vince pushed her gently to the side with a sigh.

She was passed out cold, and thankfully so. There was no way he was going to take advantage of her in her drunken state. With the feeling of her body against his, he knew he was in for a sleepless night.

•

The sounds of seagulls outside cawing in the morning sun woke Morgan up. Grinning at the warm body under hers, she felt him move and opened her eyes slightly.

She was having a marvelous dream, and it hadn't dawned on her yet that the man under her was real. At least not until she raised her head and looked straight into Vince's smiling face.

Her eyes grew wild and she immediately jumped out of bed, finding herself in nothing but her undergarments. And when she pulled the blanket from the bed, she found him in nothing but his.

"No, no, no! Please tell me we didn't," she cried as she covered her body with the blanket.

Vince sat up and twisted his lips, humored at her reaction. "You mean you don't remember?"

Finding her clothes near the night stand on the floor, she hurried into the bathroom. "I can't believe this," she shouted between tears of anger as she dressed. "You had this planned all along, didn't you?"

Vince sat on the side of the bed shaking his head in amusement. "Don't worry about it. It was going to happen sooner or later."

Morgan stormed out of the bathroom and glared at him. "You took advantage of me. I trusted you."

He stood up and took her by the shoulders. "Nothing happened between us last night."

Morgan eyed him, trying to find a glimmer of truth. It was then she remembered feeling his body against hers and how good it felt. The pounding in her chest grew.

"Well, something happened, but it wasn't sex," he continued, lowering his gaze to her lips. "We had a few drinks and got to know each other a little better, that's all. Oh, and you admitted you loved me."

Morgan heaved an aggravated sigh. "I was drunk."

"I know." He chuckled at her desperation to redeem herself. "I had to carry you here last night you know."

"I don't remember that." She sat down on the bed. "I can't go out running around with you anymore, not like this."

"Why not?" he asked with a raised brow.

"Business is business, and no personal attachments. I won't get involved with another client that way." She stood up and started for the door.

Vince grabbed her by the hand. "Come on. Don't do this. What happened last night was great. You let yourself go with me and we had fun, that's all."

"It was a mistake." She jerked her arm away. "Just leave me alone from now on."

"The only reason you're acting this way is because you're starting to like me." He tossed her a cocky grin.

Although she had become quite fond of him and would be more than willing to fall back into his arms under different circumstances, she couldn't let him find a way to her heart. She just hoped it wasn't too late.

"You think you're the only one in the world who has had their heart broken?" Vince asked as she walked out the door and slammed it on him.

Damn him, she thought as she unlocked her car door. Sure, her heart had been broken a few times. Sam had sent her into an entire year of sulking, and she wasn't going to allow the chance to have that happen again.

No matter how irresistible Vince was, she would fight it.

It wasn't his entire fault though. If she hadn't been drunk and let her feelings go, she would've made it home to her own bed.

She watched Vince walk to his motorcycle as she drove through the parking lot towards the road. She caught his eye and glared at him as she pulled out onto the highway and drove away.

Mixing business with personal would never happen again. She would definitely make sure of that this time.

Chapter 4

Sliding through the snow was music to Vince's ears. It was like an electric guitar, screaming as it climbed the fret board from a low bass to an octave high. His regular stance on the snowboard felt as comfortable as a glove as he performed in front of a crowd of people standing on the side of the halfpipe watching and cheering for him.

It was his signature jump. A ten-eighty, straight into a downhill jump that made him hit the air like a jet taking off in flight. After an aerial twist mid-air with a two-handed grab, he could hear the crowd cheering loudly from the side.

When he landed on the slope, another snowboarder dressed in a yellow suit crossed his path, sending him off-balance. He fell hard to the ground and slid past the sponsor stands. Cringing as he hit the metal bar to stop himself from going over the hillside and into a group of cross-country skiers, he heard a crack and cursed loudly.

After coming to a complete stop, he reached down, brought up his board and inspected it with a raised brow. Pushing his sunglasses to the top of his head he frowned when he saw a large crack down the center of it.

"That was my favorite board," he muttered under his breath as he caught sight of the man who had knocked him down. He tucked the board under his arm and made his way to him.

"What the hell is your problem?" Vince fiercely grabbed him

by his shoulder and pushed him around. "Max." He tightened his fist, feeling the urge to punch his rival in the jaw.

"Hey now." Max chuckled in amusement. "You know we're not allowed to fight."

Vince eyed him and slowly unclenched his fist. "Always resorting to cheap tactics, aren't you?" He sneered as he walked towards the crowd near his snowmobile. "You're not worth it."

He followed Vince smugly. "Sorry you can't control the stance on your board a little better. I could show you how it's really done, but I wouldn't want to give away any of my secrets."

He snickered, balancing his sunglasses back down on his nose as Max strode in beside him. He tightened his gloves around his wrists. "We'll see who comes out on top. I'm sure it'll be just like the past few competitions, with me winning."

"You may have won the past few, but things will change," Max replied, grinning mischievously. "Your lame-ass stunts are getting boring anyway. Just about everyone can do a ten-eighty now."

Vince stopped just before his snowmobile and glared at him briefly. He wanted to punch him, but he knew it'd be another bad rap to add to his sheet. He shook his head, amused at his attempt to start a fight.

A small crowd was beginning to gather around them for autographs. Max turned his attention to two blond voluptuous women with frosted blue colored lips.

Smiling at them, he pulled both of them into his arms. They squealed as he led them to his snowmobile and sat them down, one in front of him and one behind.

Vince watched him intently. In all the amusement he got out of the guy's pitiful threats, deep down he was worried. Max had been working hard and getting better, much better. He gave credit to Max's improvement from his summer trip to the Alps.

With only a month left until the first competition of the season, he knew he had a lot of practicing to do. He only hoped he'd have his sponsors back by then.

As he neared his room in the lodge, he noticed his door was ajar. Walking carefully towards the opening, he peeked inside.

Someone sat at the bar on a stool typing on his laptop.

Unable to tell who it was by the dark coat and hood over their head, he sneaked in carefully. He wondered who could be careless enough to break into his room in the middle of the day as he inched up behind the stranger and quickly grabbed him by his arm. He slung him to the ground with a pounding thud and sneered, grinding his knee in the person's back.

It wasn't until she gave out a long, drawn-out moan he realized it wasn't a man he had wrestled to the ground—it was a woman. Turning her over carefully, he cringed when he saw her tear stricken face. Blood soiled a small cut in her lip.

"Damn it." Vince carefully pulled Morgan up to her feet.

She hunched over in pain as she tried to make her way to the couch holding her sore lip. "Are you trying to kill me?" She coughed.

He puffed out an aggravated sigh and grabbed her before she fell back over to the floor. "What the hell are you doing here?" Helping her to the couch, he pulled her jacket off of her. He sat her down and went around the counter of the open kitchen.

"I came up early." Morgan groaned as she watched him pull a first aid kit from the drawer beside the bar. "I had no idea you would be so thrilled to see me." She lay back on the couch and breathed in deeply.

"If you hadn't been on my laptop, not to mention in my room unannounced in the first place, this wouldn't have happened." He scowled as he handed her a piece of gauze.

As she held the cloth to her lip, he pulled a couch pillow from the recliner by the stone fireplace in the corner of the room. He raised her head and tucked it behind her carefully.

"Your mom gave me the key so I could get in and use the network hookup at the lodge. And that's my laptop, not yours." She glared, wincing at the pain on her lip. "I couldn't get online anyway."

He walked over to her laptop sitting on the bar. "First of all, we're up on a mountain." He chuckled as he disconnected the phone line from the back of it. "We're all satellite up here, completely wireless."

"Oh." She couldn't think of anything to say about her lack of knowledge when it came to hooking up a computer to the internet.

Within a few minutes, he had the connection configured and the web site for her e-mail refreshed. "You're all set."

Morgan got up from the couch with a groan. She walked hunched over to the bar, holding her back as if she were a ninety-nine-year-old woman without her walker, grabbing onto everything she could to make it there.

He put his hand on her shoulder. "Maybe you should lie down on the couch a little longer."

She slid onto the stool as if she were mounting a horse. "I'm fine. I just need to send an e-mail to Sally to let her know I made it."

"Sally's your business partner, right?" he asked, searching for something behind the bar.

"Yes," she answered, typing. She glanced at him when he slammed a cabinet door, obviously unable to find what he was looking for.

"Is she single?" He searched through the bottom cabinets.

"No." She curved her lips with a perturbed glance. "Why do you want to know?"

"Ah, found it." He smiled wide when he found a bottle of tequila in one of the drawers along the wall. He pulled two shot glasses from the overhead cabinet and poured the liquor into each one grinning sheepishly. "I was only curious."

She glanced at the full glass in front of her, puckering her nose. "I'm never drinking that stuff again."

"Oh, come on, just do one shot with me." He winked at her. "It's been a long day."

Morgan ignored him and returned to the e-mail she was typing to Sally, including that Vince was trying to get her drunk again at that moment. "I'll refrain."

"Suit yourself."

She eyed him closely. She'd steered clear from him since that night at the bar. Disliking the fact she had to come to the lodge early, she thought it best to forget about what happened that night and move on without a word about it. And after a month, that should've been plenty of time to mend the damage that had been done.

"Have you seen the lodge yet?" Vince leaned against the counter watching her.

"I'm here aren't I?" she answered cynically. Peering over her laptop, she watched as he capped the bottle of tequila and put it in the cabinet. She felt kind of bad for snapping at him.

Closing her laptop, she sighed with a forced grin. "I haven't seen the entire place yet." She spoke through clenched teeth.

Vince returned with a grin that was just as forced as hers. "Well then, let me show you around."

•

The day was refreshing. Without a cloud in the sky, it was the perfect image of a crisp autumn day. A cool breeze rustled golden brown leaves to the ground, blanketing patches of green grass that hadn't been covered up by snow.

Morgan had never felt so alive and invigorated as Vince led her down a straight cobblestone path surrounded with yellow and purple leaved trees, singing birds and a sunlit cove. The fall air fogged before her warm breath as she heaved a relaxing sigh.

"I should be working." She noted her thoughts, glancing at Vince as he went on about his childhood at the lodge.

"I used to sneak out here in the middle of the night." He grinned as they walked into a garden courtyard littered with dogwood and shrubs toppled with snow. They'd been planted beside a row of stone benches beautifully chiseled in a Victorian rendition.

"I'd hide my skis or snowboard underneath this bench and every night I'd come out to hit the mountain." He chuckled. "Have you ever skied at night?" He brushed off powdered snow from one of the benches and sat down.

Morgan felt awkward as she kicked the dried leaves playfully around. "I've never been skiing before."

He stared at her. "Oh, that's right."

She kept her eyes away from him, hoping she was hiding her embarrassment well. Fixing them on a nearby shack behind the garden, she slowly walked towards it, curious what was inside.

"It's all garden tools." She shrugged, hoping the last comment would dissolve into a new subject.

Vince peered over top of her, brushing his chest lightly against the back of her head. She could feel his breath near her ear and it angered her, surprisingly so.

She nervously walked back up the path towards the lodge. As she crunched through the snow, irritated he had gotten too close, she heard his footsteps behind her.

"Hold on a second," he said, catching up to her quickening pace. "If you want to learn how to ski, I'll teach you."

"I'm not interested in making this a vacation. I'm here to work." She stiffened her face coldly. "I need to find out who your last sponsors were. So if you could write them down for me as soon as possible, I'd appreciate it."

He stopped at the door, watching her stomp through the front lobby of the lodge. "You're scared."

She suddenly stopped and turned around with pursed lips. "I am not."

Her heart pounded in her chest. It wasn't the fear of learning how to ski, or the fear of taking a high ride on a lift to the top of the mountain, but it was fear of how she was starting to feel. An abrupt ending to the venture through the lodge was inevitable. Squeezing her eyes shut tight, she swallowed her feelings down and presented the cold hard stare of her business persona.

"Prancing around this place, sightseeing with tales of your past and learning to ski down some frigid mountain doesn't help me in the least." She saw anger looming in his face and lightened her scolding tone. "I just need to do the job I was hired to do. I can't do anything else. You do understand that right?"

He walked away blankly. "Whatever."

She sighed, wishing she hadn't bitten his head off. It was better she stay as far away as humanly possible from him. She knew it could turn into Sam all over again if she let her feelings go.

She went to her room and changed into a comfortable pair of sweats, her oversized sweatshirt and favorite Yankees ball cap. Retrieving her laptop from Vince's room, she decided to work in the lobby of the lodge. It was quiet, had a beautiful stone fireplace that roared and crackled with a cozy fire, and fortunately had the most beautiful view of the mountains on the horizon. Although distracting in a sense, it helped her visualize her outline a little better.

Vince. He was an expert snowboarder, downhill speed skier and an all-around athlete. He was also a troublemaker in small handfuls, and handsome enough to get the most beautiful women in bed with him.

Sorting the good things from the bad things he'd been involved with, she was glad to see the pros outweighed the cons. Sadly, sponsors had been sending him letters that they were dropping him for obvious reasons. Even new sponsors had turned him down due to hearsay about his troublemaking.

Morgan read one of the letters, frustrated by their ignorance.

•

Dear Mr. Evans,

We have decided to decline your renewal of sponsorship due to your poor attitude and failure to show up to company benefits. We don't believe you have the proper etiquette for the Olympic atmosphere.

Regards,
Mr. Schultz,
President of Ski Running Publications

•

"How degrading," Morgan thought aloud. She wondered what Vince had done to deserve a letter so negative, as well as about a dozen others that had been written in a similar fashion.

"Hello."

Morgan glanced up to see who was speaking to her. A handsome blond, blue-eyed man sat across from her on the couch with his nose in a *Ski Running Magazine.*

Morgan smiled. "Hi."

They exchanged glances briefly, grinning. Feeling a little flush by his obvious crush on her, she went back to her thoughts on Vince.

He truly needed her, and she hoped he would cooperate with the ideas swirling in her head. Each one was typed into a notepad and saved into a folder on her desktop.

"You don't look like you're on a vacation." The man interrupted her thoughts again, tossing her another award-winning glance.

Morgan shifted her weight away from the fire. "No, I rarely have time for luxuries." She smiled back as he lowered the magazine from his face.

Beautiful, she thought. "Probably gay," she mumbled under her breath, returning her gaze to the bright blue screen of her laptop.

"What did you say?" he asked, setting down the magazine on the oak end table beside him, almost knocking off the silver moose lamp sitting there.

She struggled for an answer. "I said it's a beautiful day." Glancing outside, she realized it had grown dark and the horizon was a hazy shade of lavender. "Or, it *was* a beautiful day."

She couldn't believe how late it had gotten to be. She'd worked the entire day without any lunch, and it was already past seven. Her stomach growled, and she blushed.

"Would you join me in the restaurant for a little dinner?" The man chuckled at the rumble.

Morgan inspected his face. He looked innocent enough. She had plenty of experience with the "so good they're bad" kind of guy. But she was starving and the restaurant was very open and public.

"I'd love to." She stretched out her hand for him to shake. "My name's Morgan."

The man took her hand in his and pulled her up to her feet.

"Max." He flashed a grin she thought could be a superhero

smile with a sparkling gleam. "Max Richards."

"It's nice to meet you."

He led her down the hallway to the restaurant. And within moments, they were sitting down at a nice bistro table beside a large pane window.

"It's lovely here."

"Yes, it is," Max replied as the waiter came to the table.

He ordered without looking at the menu. He was obviously a regular at the lodge. She wondered if he knew Vince.

As she glanced at the menu items, she eyed one dish in particular. Getting a kick out of Vince's favorite Chicken Parmesan with a double twist of lemon, she cracked a grin and ordered it. Max eyed her keenly.

"So, do you know him?" he asked.

Morgan gave the menu to the waiter and returned her attention to Max. "Do I know who?"

"You ordered a Vince dish," he said smugly.

She couldn't help but snicker at the way he said it. It sounded positively inane.

The waiter returned with two wine glasses and a bottle. The moment was quiet as he poured red wine for them and then left with a smile.

"I'm so hungry I could eat the menu," she said as she pulled in the red wine from her glass.

"They always have excellent food here," Max said.

Morgan grinned. "It's hard to get a table at a good restaurant in the city. So this will be a treat if the food is good here."

He acted surprised. "Oh, you're from the city?"

"New York, born and raised," she said as she folded her arms on the table. "Go Yanks."

Max laughed. It wasn't just a complimentary laugh either. It was genuine, real in a sense that he was enjoying her company. She hadn't felt that from a man in a long while.

"So, are you from the city?"

He shook his head. "Oh, no, at least not New York anyway. I'm a Philly boy."

The waiter came back to their table carrying three steaming plates of food. Morgan's mouth watered as she eyed the small browned crab cakes in the center of the table. Garnished with lemon wedges, tartar sauce and a couple of sprigs of parsley, they looked divine.

She smiled when she took a bite. "Oh, that's good."

"I told you they were excellent." He grinned, plunging his cake into the boat of sauce.

She sipped on her red wine and began to eat. The sweet bitter flavor accented the parmesan chicken perfectly, she thought.

He glanced at her after every bite he took. She felt a little uncomfortable with his stare, but only in hopes he wouldn't see sauce dripping down her chin.

She smiled. "So you know the family that owns this place?"

"Only too well," he widened his eyes as if he'd been offended and took a bite of the linguini he'd been picking through since it arrived at their table.

He nodded as he chewed daintily on what she thought was air instead of food. Intrigued, she leaned in to ask him how he knew them, but was interrupted by a low growl behind her.

"Max."

Morgan's eyes widened when she recognized Vince's voice. She sat as still as she could, hoping he wouldn't see it was her. She was glad she'd left her hat on.

"I didn't know you dated women?" Vince chuckled.

She couldn't figure out what worried her most, the fact he was starting a fight with someone she'd just met, or that he might fight her if he found out she was listening in without him realizing who she was. But this was a first-hand witness to his troublemaking side.

"Vince, I was just talking about your family." Max continued to take smiling bites of his food as if nothing was wrong.

Vince eyed Morgan, or rather the back of her head, without a clue to who she was. "Watch out for this one, he's a sly one."

Morgan nodded her head, accepting the warning, but didn't speak a word. Her palms were sweating. Squeezing the fork tightly, she watched as he sat down in the back with some blond, cleavage-hung gorgeous woman.

Morgan lowered her eyes into a glare and started to eat again, forcing food into her mouth. She couldn't figure out why she was getting angry at Vince, no doubt flirting profusely with the vixen he was with. By the way the woman giggled she was surprised she didn't just duck underneath the table for him.

With that thought, Morgan choked, losing her breath. Coughing loudly, she tucked her head to her knees as Max ran around the table and pounded on her back.

"Are you okay?"

She had to leave the dining area to gain control. Angry at him and angry with herself for being jealous, she ran out into the hallway.

Hanging on the wall near the flight of stairs that led to the rooms, she bent over and finally coughed up the piece of noodle that had caused her scene. She breathed hard, catching her breath.

Max finally came out after being stalled into paying the dinner bill. "Are you okay now?" He smiled with his hand on Morgan's shoulder.

She nodded. "I'm fine. I just choked a little."

"I see that." He chuckled.

"Thank you so much for dinner. But I think I might just retire for the rest of the night." Morgan started up the stairs, but was stopped by Max's hand.

"You mind if I walk you?" He tossed his well-feathered hair from his eyes and curved his arm for Morgan to take. "I mean, just in case you lose your balance on the stairs."

She let out a brief sigh. She wasn't sure she wanted to be bothered anymore after her embarrassing performance. But she grinned graciously and looped her arm through his. "Sure, why not."

He walked her to her room and leaned on the wall while she unlocked the door. "Feel like company?"

Morgan smiled as she stood in the open doorway. "I'm sorry

Max. It was very nice to meet you, but I have work to finish tonight."

He tossed her a playful frown. "It's so sad a beautiful woman like you is working instead of having fun." He turned away from the door. "I'll see you around then."

"Thanks again for dinner," she called out as he started back down the stairs.

She closed the door behind her with a relieved sigh. "What was I thinking?" She scolded herself as she walked to the wool blanketed bed.

She sat down heavily. Bouncing up and down, she bit her lower lip thinking about how Vince might have reacted if he'd seen her with Max. Would he have been as jealous as she was for seeing him with another woman?

She lay back on the bed and turned out the light. After a few moments, she heard a man and a woman's voice moaning as a knocking sound played against the wall.

She covered her ears with pillows from the blue recliner in the corner of the room, but it didn't seem to help. The sounds just grew louder.

Unable to take it any longer, she left her room with a fast slam of the door behind her. She huffed angrily and walked down the stairs to the lobby. It was quiet except for the constant dinging of arcade noises coming from the room past the restaurant, which was now closed.

She found a family inside playing games against each other. The young boy, who was at least twelve, pulled at his father's shirt trying to get his attention.

"Come on, Dad. You promised you would take me snowboarding tonight."

"We're going tomorrow night, son."

Morgan watched in awe and a strange idea began to work through her brain. She left the room, walking in a daze as she thought of how Vince could restore his reputation. Entwined with a lot of coordination, and hopefully his cooperation, she thought her idea was wonderful.

She went back to her room and closed the door with a grin. Happy that her sex-crazed neighbors had ended their noise, she began to sketch out the outline of her brilliant plan to win him back his sponsors.

•

"What's this?" Morgan thought aloud as she stepped out into the hallway outside her door the next morning and found a note folded on the floor. She reached down to retrieve it and just as she picked it up, Vince's door swung open.

The woman who had been with Vince at dinner was leaving the room with a frown. Her makeup was smeared and her dress was ripped at the shoulder as she slammed the door and scampered off down the hallway in tears.

Morgan was appalled. Still wearing her pink long john pajamas, she stomped to Vince's door and pounded on it. It wasn't Vince who answered.

"Who are you?" A handsome young man with dark spiked hair opened the door.

"I could ask the same thing?" Morgan snapped, trying to peer inside. "Where's Vince?"

The young man smiled. "He flew to Mom and Dad's house last night."

"He flew?"

"Yeah, he took the helicopter. What did you think I meant?" He chuckled.

"I didn't know there was a helicopter. And I didn't know Vince could fly."

He laughed again. "Nah, the pilot flew him. The name's Chad," he said, running his eyes down her body with a grin. "Nice PJs."

"I'm Morgan."

"Oh yeah, Vince told me about you." Another snort came from him as if there was a hidden joke there somewhere.

She lowered her brow and shot him a cynical glance. "So when is he due back?"

"Good morning."

Morgan twisted around and found Vince standing behind her

with the usual smirk on his face. *Brothers indeed,* she thought.

"Chad man, it's good to see you." Vince shook his brother's hand like it was some secret handshake. "Sorry I had to jet on you and your girlfriend last night."

"I broke it off with her, man. She told me this morning she slept with some guy last weekend while I was out of town."

"Ah man, sorry to hear that."

Vince stared at her, eyeing her pink pajamas. She eyed him back, almost forgetting what she had come over to talk to him about until she followed him into the room.

"Are you sleeping well? Your eyes are dark," he asked her, taking off his jacket.

"No, besides the fact I can hear everything that goes on in this room at night." She glared at Chad with an evil eye. "But that's not the only reason I was up all night. I was working on a plan to help build your reputation with the sponsors."

She sat down on the black soft leather couch in front of the fireplace and waited for a response. She watched as Vince grabbed an orange juice from the refrigerator and chugged it down as if she hadn't said a word.

Chad made his way to the shower, leaving them alone to talk. He sat down beside her, but closed his eyes as if he were going to sleep.

"Didn't you hear a word I said?"

"Yeah, I'm waiting on you to tell me about it," he mumbled keeping his eyes closed.

An awkward silence rang in her ears as anger crept back up into her face. "Just acknowledge me once in awhile, let me know that you're actually listening."

Vince opened his eyes and turned his head to her. "I'm listening."

"Are you sure?" she asked.

"I'd turn my ear towards you, but you might think I wasn't listening because I'm not looking at you. So I guess I have to keep my eyes on you to let you know I'm listening." He smiled again, but this time she couldn't help but find humor in it.

"Ah, do I hear laughter?" He stared into her eyes as she continued to laugh.

"Stop that." Morgan pushed him playfully on his shoulder.

"Oh, you want to fight do you?" He touched her lightly on her ribs, making her laugh again.

"I don't like being tickled." She went to the floor, followed by his wandering hands tickling her in all the right places. "Go away!" she shouted between snorts of laughter.

"Dem are fightin' words." He pulled her up to the couch and over top of him.

She suddenly found herself in a compromising situation. Leaning her body on his, he pulled her down to his lips and kissed her.

She hated it and enjoyed it at the same time. It was tender, swept-off her-feet exciting, and a completely stupid thing to do.

"No." She pulled away from him with a scowl. "We can't go there."

Vince sighed, sitting himself up on the couch and stretching his legs down the length of it. "Why do you give yourself rules? It's the silliest thing I've ever heard."

She grabbed the note she'd dropped on the floor and started towards the door. Disgusted by giving in to him so easily, she let out an aggravated sigh.

"Wait," he called out. "You never told me your idea."

Morgan turned back around and lowered her brows in anger. "When you're ready to listen, I mean seriously listen, I'll tell you."

"Look." He put his hands behind his back, flashing an innocent smile. "I'm listening."

Morgan sighed. The excitement about her plans had passed and was taken over by an urge to hop back on the couch with him and let rule number one be broken, just once.

"I thought we could organize a kids' weekend here. Where they compete in a junior competition in which the winner would receive a grand prize of a free weekend here and free snowboarding lessons from you on an autographed new snowboard." Morgan said it with feeling enough to put a horse to sleep. "Hence, all the named sponsors would be invited here to witness your new and improved niceness in which they would happily renew your sponsorship. That's the plan," she added as she walked out the door.

Damn, Morgan, she thought. *Break the rules and throw him a run-on sentence at that. He's really digging your professional skills.* She groaned as she headed to her room.

She'd almost forgotten about the unread note in her hand and unfolded it to some very nice handwriting. It was from Max.

"Morgan, thanks for dinner last night. I hope we can do it again soon on a more formal setting. Tonight maybe? I'll stop by."

Rolling her eyes, she stumbled into her room. Exhausted, embarrassed and hoping she could get at least a few hours of sleep, she fell back on her bed.

But when she closed her eyes, Vince's luscious lips reached for hers, stretching aimlessly towards her mouth. His stare bore into her own as she watched him inch closer, mesmerizing her into a trance. Engulfing in the most fantastic, erotic kiss she'd ever experienced, she let him pull her into his arms. But when they began to roll together like a croc consuming its victim, she suddenly opened her eyes.

Holding her head to her temple at even the slightest thought of Vince invading her dreams, she got up from the bed. She walked to the small kitchenette and poured her a glass of water from the faucet, still feeling quite ill with excitement.

She hated this. Here she was, still in her pajamas daydreaming about one of the worst things she could possibly do. It was his fault for doing this to her.

Moaning, she set the glass down on the counter and dragged her feet back to the bed. She tripped over her shoes and fell onto the soft mattress just as a knock came on the door.

It startled her. She hesitated for a moment to get up and answer, but the thought she'd miss out on something important outweighed her depression.

With a heaving groan, she got up and opened the door to

Vince's smiling face. "What do you want?"

"Hey." He leaned on the side of the doorway.

Morgan went to the bed and lay back down, trying to keep her last images of him from popping back up. "Like I said, what do you want?"

"Listen." He walked in and closed the door. "I like your idea."

Morgan slowly sat up, running her fingers through her messed up hair. Awakened with growing excitement that finally she had him ready to cooperate with her, a smile escaped her lips.

"Really?"

"Yeah," he said with a nod.

Morgan grinned. "Are you serious?"

"Sure. I think it's a good idea, but I don't want to do it. I'm not donating my extra time for any kids. I have plenty of things to keep me busy right now. Practicing needs to be my priority." His face soured into a slight frown. "It's not that I don't like kids. I love them actually. It's just what you suggested is a bit too much of a hassle, don't you think?"

"Why do you say that?" She frowned at him.

"There's just not enough time to set up something of that stature. It's too big for you to do alone."

"Ye of little faith," she argued. "I've set up sold-out concerts in Olympic-size stadiums in a matter of weeks. With the proper handle on this, I could have it set up in no time."

"My answer is no." The evil eye shined under his dark brows.

"I am going to set this up."

"No, you're not."

"Yes, I am."

"Morgan."

"Vince."

A moment of silence passed as they glared at each other. The tension was as thick as molasses, but neither of them would back down.

"If you do this—" Morgan eased her glare. "I swear I won't bother you with helping. All you'll have to do is show up."

With an aggravated huff, he turned on his heels and left the room. She slumped down into the bed. She wondered if she was losing her aggressive touch.

He had to understand she knew what was best for his career. After all, that's why they'd hired her. Emma would make it happen, even if he didn't want it.

She let out an exasperated sigh. But if he didn't attend his own event, his reputation would drown for sure. And when it had something to do with influential children, a circus of media and sponsors that already thought him to be a lost cause, well then—he'd *better* show up.

Chapter 5

Glancing in the rear view mirror of her car, Morgan smiled at her reflection. She had dressed herself up to make an impression with the sports crowd at Joe's Bar. And although she promised herself she wouldn't do this again, she was looking forward to hanging out with Vince.

She only hoped her surprise visit with him wouldn't backfire. It was all part of the plan to sweet talk him into agreeing to the junior competition that was already set and ready to go.

Armed in a casual black mini-skirt with a white stripe down each side, a white spandex tank underneath a black hooded sweat-shirt, she got out of her car.

She searched the parking lot as she walked towards the entrance and spotted his dark blue truck shining underneath the street light. A smile escaped her lips.

She nervously walked into the crowded room. People seemed livelier than they were the last time she was there. The music from the jukebox was loud and there were actually people dancing on the dance floor.

As she mingled through towards the bar, she searched the room. The hiatus of maturity seemed to fall amongst everyone tonight. Women and men laughed energetically over each other as techno blared throughout the room.

It was stimulating. Every bit of her will to keep to her mission of finding Vince in the crowded room seemed to get tossed out the window as she began to dance with everyone else.

Grinning at the opportunity to finally let loose from her stagnant business guise, she let her hair down from the clip that held it in place. She found her hips moving provocatively as she stepped with the rhythm, grinning in fascination as others moved with her in the same manner.

Trance beats seemed to dance with her underneath the strobe lights. Blending colors, fast transitions, the atmosphere bellowed out a good time, and she was right smack-dab in the middle of it.

A pair of hands found her hips and a body moved with her from behind. The familiar but faint aroma of cologne filled her nostrils and she knew exactly who it was.

She suddenly felt his lips on her ear, but couldn't bring herself to pull away. After all, it was just a dance and she was having too good of a time to worry about it.

"What are you doing here?" Vince shouted.

He stumbled slightly when she turned around to face him, but it was purposely done to have her catch his arms in her hands.

"I came to have a little fun."

"You came to find me, didn't you?"

A smirk broke out across his face when she suddenly glared at him. She slid her hands down his arms and removed his hands from her hips. She walked towards the bar eager for him to follow so they could talk.

With Vince right behind her, she found an empty stool and sat down. The upbeat music ended abruptly and a slow country song began to play. In unison, the crowd booed the selection and one by one they left the dance floor.

Joe shook his head in amusement at the negative reaction as he came to stand in front of Morgan. "What can I get you tonight?"

"Still no wine?" she asked, ignoring Vince's staring.

Joe shook his head. "Sorry. How about I make you a margarita?"

"Sure." She finally acknowledged Vince who had suddenly turned his attention to a football game, obviously not wanting her to catch him looking.

"Hey stranger," said a familiar voice from the other side of her.

She turned to meet Max who was flashing his brilliant superhero smile. "Hey Max. How are you?"

"I'm good." He sat down on the stool, bottle of beer in hand and gave her his full attention.

Vince leaned back and peered around Morgan who had begun to panic. "What are you doing?" Vince asked him with a perturbed growl.

"I was just saying hi to a friend," Max answered. "What are you doing?"

Morgan pitched her gaze forward nervously and watched them in the mirrored wall behind the shelf of liquor. As if they were in a staring contest, they sneered at each other, their eyes meeting behind her back.

"You know him?" Vince asked her, pointing his index finger rigidly at him as he stared at the side of her head.

With her eyes still fixed on his reflection, she smiled. "Yeah, I met him at the lodge."

The frown on his lips matched his glowering eyes as he looked at Max again. Jealousy. It was such a strange emotion coming from a man who didn't seem to care much about her, at least not in that kind of way. Sadly, she kind of liked it.

"She was choking, so I helped her," Max added to her answer.

Vince relaxed his brows. With a quick nod, he backed down from a possible argument and returned his attention back to the television.

Not knowing if it was the margarita or if she was curious he really was jealous, she turned her body to Vince. She nervously cleared her throat.

"I had dinner with him at the restaurant that night you were with Chad's girlfriend. You walked by and didn't bother to see it was me he was with." She shrugged. "I had your Parmesan dish, which was actually quite good, but I choked on one of the noodles. Max here saved me."

Getting a kick out of his stunned reaction, she turned around to face Max. "I meant to repay you for buying me dinner. Let me buy you a beer."

"Thanks." He beamed, elbowing her playfully. "Listen, I'll have to show you some of the views around the lodge sometime. There's this one place where it seems you can see the entire sky."

"Sounds intriguing," she answered, smiling playfully.

She tried to ignore Vince's grip on her elbow, but the persistence of his gentle squeezes had grown into light tugs. Leaving Max's gaze, she turned her attention back to his angry face.

"What are you doing?" he asked through clenched teeth. "You shouldn't be around him."

"He's just a friend, Vince." She grinned, trying not to show the enjoyment she was getting out of his jealousy.

"He's just using you to get to me. That's how he works." He glanced at Max, who had turned his attention to a young woman on the other side of him, then fixed his eyes back on Morgan. "Trust me. You don't want to get mixed up with him."

"What is it with you two?" she asked. Finishing off her margarita, she swiveled in the stool to face him and tried to ignore that her knees were touching his leg. "I can understand you're rivals on the slopes, but it seems your hatred for him goes deeper than that."

Vince sighed. He turned back towards the bar, blankly staring at the empty beer bottle in his hand.

"Well, if you can't tell me why you don't want me talking to him, then I have no choice but to ignore your concern."

"You never answered my question."

"What question?" She stared at him, puzzled as to why he couldn't talk to her seriously.

"Why you came here tonight?"

"Oh." Morgan suddenly grinned.

The mischievous expression on her face made him interested in what she had to say. The cockiness returned to his eyes as he stared at her, patiently awaiting her reply.

"Your mother is funding the competition for the kids." Morgan refused to look at him. "I've already contacted all the media and sponsors. They agreed to do speed coverage to advertise the event."

Vince shook his head and sighed. "Damn it, Morgan. I told you I wasn't interested."

"It's already in motion. You have no choice but to accept it," she said as she waved Joe over to her. "I think you'll be happy about a sponsor I picked up recently."

"By the look on his face, I see you've told him about our agreement." Joe grinned auspiciously, setting another margarita down in front of her.

Vince raised his eyes to Joe. "Don't tell me you're in on this?"

Joe held out his arms and smiled. "You're looking at your new, most dedicated sponsor."

Morgan graciously accepted the salted glass in her hand and raised it to her lips. She would've enjoyed the moment, but someone let out an infuriating sigh. At first she thought it was Vince ready to cause a fuss. But when Max stood up from his stool and slammed his beer down on the bar, she flinched.

"What the hell, Joe?" Max spat out angrily. "I've been asking you for sponsorship for over a year now."

"Sorry, Max," Joe shrugged. "You've been making some rather poor judgments lately. I can't risk ruining my name and business on someone like you."

"What have I done that's so terrible?" He glanced at Vince who was watching, intently waiting to go to bat for his friend if needed. Max grinned over his anticipation.

Morgan was shocked by his reaction. She hadn't realized Max had been trying to get sponsorship from him, too. Otherwise she wouldn't have brought it up with him there.

"Let it go, Max," she said in an apologetic voice. She lightly touched his arm with her hand. "I didn't mean for it to upset you. I had no idea ... "

Max jerked his arm away and glared at her. "It's not your fault." He gathered his beer in his hand and angrily walked off.

Morgan started to go after him, but Vince grabbed her hand and pulled her back down in her seat. The concern in her eyes was prominent as she stared after him.

"Don't worry about him," Joe said, gathering her attention. "He's a hothead, but he'll get over it eventually."

"Just stay away from him," Vince added. "He's not exactly on the straight and narrow."

"What do you mean?" she asked.

Vince glanced around to make sure nobody was listening, and leaned in close to her. "He's getting into some serious trouble recently. He was seen at a party reading lines, if you know what I mean."

Morgan had heard that saying before. She could see it easily with musicians, but a professional athlete was mostly unheard of, looked down upon. It was no wonder Joe didn't want to sponsor him, if the rumor was even true about him.

Her cell phone suddenly rang. The chime played Regina's disco song, and her mind soared happily to hear from her friend.

"Hello." She grinned, excusing herself from the bar and from Vince's perplexed stare.

"Morgan," Regina said—followed by some incoherent mumbles of words she couldn't understand.

"Hold on," she said as she made her way to the restroom.

She walked in the door and leaned against the counter. Surprised there were only a few women primping in the mirrors instead of packed in like the usual can of sardines, she returned her attention to the call.

"Sally wants you to come into the office in the morning. She needs you to bring your plans for the competition so we can get some commercials set up for the local stations."

"Okay. I'll be there around ten."

As one of the women left the bathroom, she turned to take a look at herself in the mirror. Cringing at her reflection, she picked at a curled lock of hair sticking up in the back.

"I also want you to know I might be quitting." Regina sighed.

"What?" Morgan was shocked to hear it.

"I'm thinking about moving back to Seattle to be near my mother."

"Oh Regina, I'll miss you if you leave." She thought for a moment as she straightened another lock of hair from her eyes. "If you need more money, I'm sure I can work in a nice raise for you."

Tired of fussing with her uncooperative hair, she turned and leaned back against the counter again. About to continue pleading with her to rethink her possible decision, she was interrupted by the bathroom door.

It swung open and a woman fled inside with a look of panic. Her eyes caught Morgan's and a big smirk escaped her open mouth.

"The cops are here!" she exclaimed. "They're hauling someone's ass to jail for starting a bar fight."

"I'll call you later, Regina."

With her mouth agape, Morgan hung up and brushed past the woman. She stormed out of the bathroom and down the hallway just in time to see the police escort Vince, in handcuffs, out the front door.

"What the hell?" she whispered under her breath as she pushed through the gawking crowd towards the bar where Joe was standing with a disgusted look.

Max sat in the stool talking to a policeman. Holding a cup of ice to his jaw, he turned to face her as she came to stand beside him in awe.

"What happened?" she asked Max, glancing at the cop who gave her a stern eye.

"Just come down to the station to give an official statement." The policeman started to walk away, but turned back around. "I'd suggest you take a cab tonight, or you'll end up in a cell with your buddy. That goes for you too, young lady."

Morgan watched him walk through the separating crowd and out the entrance door. She turned to Max and inspected his jaw. The small cut on his lip was barely noticeable, although blood was imminently beading on it. A bruise showed faintly on his chin, but it didn't look bad.

She lowered her brows, looking at Joe. "What happened?"

"Ask the idiot here." Joe nodded towards Max.

Holding his jaw, Max stood up and started for the door. Morgan followed him out and into the parking lot before he turned to her.

"Your boy has a mean right hook." He chuckled. Seeing that Morgan wasn't finding humor in it, he lowered the icy cup from his jaw. "I guess I went a little too far. Sometimes I can be a little immature."

"What did you do?" she asked, watching him pull out a set of keys from his pocket. They were keys to Vince's truck.

Max handed them to her and smiled painfully. "I was just messing with him and took his keys. I threatened to take you out on a date in his truck, and that's when he—" His voice trailed as he nonchalantly reenacted the punch for her.

"That's just great, Max." Morgan pulled the keys from his grasp and headed towards the truck with him following her. "If it gets out now he was arrested for another bar fight, the event could be ruined."

Frantic to get to the police station, she hopped up inside the truck. As she started the engine, Max opened the passenger door and leapt up inside.

"What are you doing?" she asked.

"I'm going to the station to give my statement." He grinned. "You're going there anyway, so you can give me a ride."

"Get out of the truck."

"I'm sure you won't mind me riding once you listen to my suggestion on how to deal with this."

She thought for a moment. Seeing that he wasn't going to budge, she shifted the truck into drive and pulled out of the parking lot.

"So what is it?" she asked, trying not to sound hateful towards him.

"I have a simple proposition," he said, throwing her his typical obtuse and mischievous smile. "I won't press charges if you agree to go out with me."

Morgan laughed. "You want me to go out with you?"

"On a date, that is all. If you want your boy out of trouble, you'll agree."

What ulterior motives he had, she thought as they pulled up to the curb in front of the police station and parked. There was definitely something up his sleeve, but she was too hard up on Vince's career right now to turn down the offer.

"Fine," she answered. "I'll go out with you on one date, but only as a friend. The truth is that I do like you Max, but you have a tendency to rub people the wrong way, especially Vince."

Max arched his brows and smiled. "I'm glad you said that."

"Said what?"

"That you like me," he answered.

Shaking her head in amusement, she stepped down out of the truck. She met Max on the other side and they both headed up the steps to the front door of the precinct.

After a few moments, a man in a dark blue uniform came to get them. He led them back to the main room and to his desk along the back wall.

With a pen in hand, he frowned at Max as he sat down in his chair. "You're the one from the bar fight at Joe's?" he asked.

"Yes," Max answered.

"How much have you had to drink tonight?"

Max thought for a few seconds and then smiled. "I've had maybe four beers."

"You took a cab here right?" He eyed him carefully.

"Of course," Max lied, glancing at Morgan.

"So in your own words, exactly what happened?"

Max threw him an award-winning smile. "Listen sir, I've decided I don't want to press charges. It seems it would upset my lady friend here, and I definitely don't want to do that."

The policeman immediately threw his pen down on his desk. At first, Morgan thought he was angry for wasting his time, but when he stood up with a sudden grin, she could tell he was the total opposite.

"It takes a big man to drop charges after he's been assaulted. Let's go release your friend." He glanced at the both of them and motioned them to follow, and like clockwork, they stood up and complied.

"Wait," Max said, stopping suddenly. He turned his attention to Morgan and winked. "I'm going to let you do this, dear."

"Okay," she answered, happy he'd made that decision.

"I'll get with you on that date you owe me though, so don't forget about it."

Morgan rolled her eyes as he walked away. She began to wonder if he pretended to be happy with everything around him, and really was a tormented soul. It was a little frightening to think he could star in his own horror movie with just him standing on the screen smiling.

She shivered slightly as she followed the policeman through a door in the back. Awing at the cells as she passed them, her body began to tremble.

The policeman stopped at the last cell and began to unlock it, but Morgan stopped him with her hand. He glanced at her, and seeing the look in her eyes, he nodded he understood and left the two of them alone.

She walked forward and peered inside. Vince sat on the floor, back to wall with his wrists dangling over his knees, looking at her smugly between his parted legs.

It was strange. His bad-boy look aroused her in a way she'd never felt before. It wasn't exactly the sensation she'd wanted when she bitched him out for getting arrested, but she'd have to make do with it.

"So you came to bail me out?" he asked, rising to his feet.

"No."

She watched him walk towards her. The half-grin he wore as he looped his fingers around the bars made her wish she'd kept her eyes away. He was too sexy to get an earful, but she had to swallow down her emotions and give him a little bit of a scolding.

"Are you trying to ruin all the work I've put into you?" she said, pushing her flushed sensation away with a glare.

"I already have a mother," he growled.

She let out a short laugh through her nose. "So you do."

"Just get me out of here."

The policeman came back and unlocked the door. "I'm sorry ma'am. I'm going to have to ask that you guys go ahead and leave. They need the box for real criminals." He watched Vince pass him as he walked out of the cell. "Stay out of trouble. You got lucky this time, and I doubt you'll get another chance if it happens again."

Ignoring the cop's attempt to give him advice, he walked towards the door. With Morgan following him, they made their way out to the truck.

"So if you didn't post bail, who did?" he asked as he held his hand out for his keys.

"Max decided not to press charges."

She walked around to the driver's side. She leapt up into the truck and sat there waiting for him to get in. It took a moment, but he finally caved and hopped inside.

"What made him decide not to press charges? The guy's been out to get me for a long time. I figured this was his chance to really put a hurt on me."

Morgan started the engine and pulled out onto the road. She really didn't want to tell him about the deal she made with Max, but she was sure he'd find out anyway. With the big mouth Max carried around on him, it was inevitable.

She bit her lower lip, unsure how to put it. Feeling his stare on her face, nervousness entrapped her.

"I told him—" she paused, thinking of the words to say. "I agreed to go out on *one* date with him, as a friend only. He told me if I did, he wouldn't press charges."

"Turn this damn truck around!" he shouted angrily. "I'd rather spend the weekend in jail than watch you go out with him."

"Don't get your panties in a wad," she argued, grinning at her choice of words. "I'm a big girl. I can make my own decisions."

"You don't understand Morgan. I don't want you out alone with him. He's my rival, and not just in sports, if you catch my drift." He let out an aggravated sigh as they pulled into the bar parking lot. "He's not as friendly as you think."

Morgan parked beside her car and turned the engine off. She twisted her body towards him and propped her knee up on the truck's bench seat, dangling her ankle over the edge.

"I can take care of myself," she said. "It's just one outing with him. I wouldn't even call it a date. Plus, it's for the sake of your career. I've done worse for my job, some unmentionable things I don't want to go into, but I'd do them again to keep my client out of trouble."

"When you say unmentionable things—" he stuttered, surprised she'd said something like that.

She tittered at his reaction. "Wow, you really think well of me. Do you believe I'd turn tricks for a job?"

"Sure sounded like it to me by the way you put it."

"I'm not like that, Vince, so you can stop worrying about it."

"What kind of unmentionables then?" he asked. A grin slowly crept across his face and he arched his brows in curiosity. "Maybe you were with women instead?"

Seeing that he was suddenly getting a kick out of his sick sense of humor, she opened the door and hopped out. She slammed the truck door as he quickly got out and rounded the front to meet her before she could unlock her car door.

"Hey. I'm sorry," he said as he came to stand behind her. "Sometimes I can be a real jerk."

"You think?" She glared at him hatefully.

He grasped her shoulders gently and turned her around to face him. With pursed lips, he gave her a serious eye.

"Please, I'm begging you to stay away from him. I'm telling you, he's bad news."

"I really appreciate the concern, but it's just one simple evening."

An awkward silence swirled around them. Morgan thought for sure he'd lean down and kiss her, and for some reason she'd allow it. But he let go of her shoulders and leaned back away.

"Just think about what I'm asking," he said. "If you go out with him, there'd be nobody there to protect you if he tried anything."

"Vince." She smiled sweetly as she put her hand on his shoulder. "I appreciate your concern. And the fact you're so into this chivalry type thing is commendable, but we're in another century. Women are stronger than men give them credit for. Stop trying to protect me and please, please stop arguing with me over this."

He shook his head at her comment and turned away. He opened the truck door, glancing at her coolly. And as he hopped up inside he frowned.

"It doesn't matter if you think I'm being overprotective or not, I'm just giving you my word of warning that if you do this, you'll regret it."

He turned on the engine and rolled down the window. With a quick pull, he shut the truck door, waited until she got in her car and started it. She rolled her window down to get one last word in, but he beat her to the punch.

"I'll see you at the lodge."

"See you later," she said as he watched him drive away.

As she took off down the road toward her house, a little voice inside told her to listen to what he'd said, that she should back out of the deal.

But she couldn't let Vince's career take another hit in the wrong direction, not now that it was finally beginning to take off.

Chapter 6

Morgan didn't think it would happen, but Vince actually showed up to the event. She smiled as she watched him do his stunts in front of the crowd sitting in the stands on the side of the half-pipe.

She could tell all the kids loved it when they went wild over his signature jump. They were screaming her thoughts exactly. She also knew how much he loved showing off in front of them.

He was agile on his board. The performance he gave was perfect, a show-stopper. The way he looked, the way he walked, the way he smiled—he was magnificent. If only she were a spectator instead of his manager, she'd do many things to him afterwards. And if only she hadn't thought about those things, she wouldn't be blushing now.

Behind the judge's podium was a small section for the people she had invited specifically. Editors from popular ski magazines, reporters from the newspapers and television stations, sports broadcasters and a handful of merchant sponsors littered the seats awing at his spectacular moves. They made it out to be a more important day for Vince than for the kids that were determined to win the grand prize.

"This actually turned out better than I expected," Morgan heard one of the sponsors say as she passed underneath the stands and found a seat near the bottom row.

"Mr. Evans seems to be doing well these days," another one

commented, followed by a mumbled agreement from the rest of them.

Morgan shivered in delight at the thought of Vince finally getting gratitude instead of negativity. He deserved it. He may not show interest in it most of the time, but she knew he was definitely heading towards stardom.

Fixing her eyes forward, she planted them on him. He was so close, sitting at the podium watching as one of the kids ran the halfpipe.

He looked good, damn good, in his black turtleneck that matched his unzipped snow coat and tossed hair. She caught herself holding her breath. He was a judge, but she thought he looked more like a teacher, the one all the schoolgirls had a crush on, preparing to go to class with his pencil stuck over his ear.

He was still upset she was going out on a date with Max. Voicing every day for the past three weeks that she shouldn't go, she began to suspect he was just trying to start an argument. It worked for the first week, but since then she ignored his comments.

Morgan took a leave from the stands. She watched as Vince made his way to the winner's podium as she ordered a hot chocolate from the concession.

This event was just a start for his real career, and she had to come up with another brilliant plan to show he'd changed his ways. Although she knew the bad situations he had been in were usually good publicity for a rock star, they definitely didn't sit well with an Olympic committee.

The sun had just begun to set. The announcer got everyone's attention near the podium beside the cotton candy vendor, hushing the noise that seemed loud enough to start an avalanche. He announced the second- and third-place winners as if he were the referee at a boxing match, which drove the crowd into relentless cheering.

Receiving medals and a small trophy, the kids smiled and waved at their nearby proud parents and the media's three ring circus of photographers. She knew this event was going to be a big hit in the future.

"Hey stranger," Max said coming up behind her and grabbing her shoulders.

With a startled grin, she turned around to greet him. "Max. I was wondering when you were going to show up."

"Are you ready for our date tonight?" he asked.

"Tonight's not a good idea," she replied, hoping Max would give up on this silly idea of obviously trying to woo her. "All of the sponsors are going to be at the party tonight, and I don't think it would be right of me to disappear."

He rolled his eyes. "Come on Morgan, you're not going back out on your word are you?"

"No," she said, pulling away from his grasp. "I'd just prefer another night. How about we go tomorrow instead? We could make it a day thing or something."

"Let me take you out tonight and treat you for a job well done." He took her by the hand and gazed into her eyes. "What you did here was amazing. God knows my manager wouldn't have been able to pull off such an event in the little time it took you." He glanced over at the crowd of people that surrounded the young boy as he held up his snowboard to Vince. "Just look at that. I'm jealous, really I am."

Morgan watched Vince sign the snowboard with a black marker followed by camera flashes and a few news reporters shooting footage of the kid's excited reaction. Vince flashed a grin and she knew he was enjoying every minute of it.

At that moment, she knew exactly how he felt. She'd seen it many times with musicians she'd brought to the top of their game. A smile curved across her face.

"Nobody is going to care if you duck out early. All the attention is going to be on him tonight."

She knew he was right. But still, she wondered what Vince would think. He was already putting down the whole idea of her going out, but to leave during his after-party might send him the wrong message. She definitely didn't want him to think she was actually interested in Max, although she already knew he was thinking it.

"I don't know." She bit her lower lip in thought.

Max sighed disappointedly. "Okay, how's this sound? There's a place up along the mountain I would love to take you to. You know, the place I told you about a few weeks ago? Do your thing with his sponsors and then we'll go." He turned her around to face him. "Just give me two hours with you and we'll call our deal even."

"Exactly why do you want to take me out so badly?" she snapped suddenly, knowing there had to be some reason for him to whisk her away to the other side of the mountain. "I mean really, do you think I'm that ignorant as to let you take me out without knowing you have some sort of plan?"

With a smile like the one Max flashed her right then, Morgan couldn't help but grin. He looked completely innocent, like the young boy who had looked at Vince while he signed his board, but Max's mischievous eyes said something else.

"Okay, the truth is I want to discuss a possible business deal with you, or rather with someone you know." He saw she was about to argue, but shushed her with a finger to her lips. "I just want you to hear what I have to say and then I'll leave you alone. Whatever your answer is, I'll accept your decision and our deal will be done."

"Why not tell me now?" she asked curiously. "Why go to all the trouble of taking me out?"

Max started to walk away, grinning back at her as he shook his head. "Tonight you owe me a date, my dear Morgan. I'll meet you out front when you're done with the party."

Morgan's attention wandered back toward Vince who was being interviewed by a television reporter. A recording device was held up to his mouth as he spoke with obvious self-confidence.

Curiosity got the better of her. Her feet crunched underneath her as she walked through the snow toward the camera lights.

"Are you going to make the Junior Snowboarding Competition an annual event after the success it had today?" the reporter asked Vince, who didn't flinch at the topic that hadn't been discussed in the slightest.

"We're coordinating efforts to continue what we think is a great opportunity for young people to come out and show off their skills." Vince smiled at the beautiful dark-haired woman.

Excellent answer, Morgan thought proudly as she listened in and watched. He was magnificent, professional and downright sexy. And in her opinion, that was news worthy of broadcasting.

"With the Winter Olympics only months away, how does it feel knowing your past may keep you from being eligible, if you're even able to qualify?"

A short silent sigh escaped Morgan's lips. Holding her breath at what Vince's answer was going to be, she clenched her gloved hands around her cup.

"My past is like you said, Ms. Sanders, in the past. There have been a lot of sports professionals who have had their share of problems, and I certainly don't think I break the mold by being the perfect model. However, I believe with my previous managers there was a lack of communication and effort put into my career. My new manager has proved herself to be hard working and determined to wring out the negativity that has stunted my opportunities. She's been a wonderful addition."

Morgan blinked in shock. It was a marvelous answer. He spoke without an awkward pause and in such a well-mannered tone that she felt like falling to her knees, especially after what he just said about her.

As the cameras quit flashing and the news crew packed up their equipment, she walked through the snow to stand in front of Vince with a smile. But before she could speak, he leaned his face in to hers with a glare.

"I saw you with Max. You're not going out with him," he said.

"You're not going to give up are you?" she asked as he started down the hill towards the lodge.

"No." He turned his head to the side as he walked. "If you go, I'll be pissed."

"You're jealous, aren't you?"

"What?" He gave out a mocking laugh and started back down

the hill with her on his heels.

"You are, admit it." She smirked. She knew she was working his nerves and for some reason she was getting pleasure out of it.

"Jealousy has nothing to do with it." He stopped again with a raised brow. "I just don't want to see you get hurt. Max isn't the guy you think he is. He's conniving and manipulative. I don't trust him, especially with the woman who's supposed to be handling my career."

"That's the reason I'm doing this, Vince," she said. "It's so he won't expose the fact you practically beat him to death."

"I hit him once." He chuckled. "I barely call that beating him to death."

"Well, whatever you want to call it. All I know is he's never done anything to hurt me, or you, since I've known him. So I don't know how you can stand there and say he's this terrible person who's going to do something completely horrific to me."

"You've only known him for a month, Morgan." He softened his face and looked down at his gloves. "Listen, you do what you want. Obviously you're not going to listen to me anyway. All I'm saying is—" He hesitated with a sigh. "Just be careful."

"Ah, so you do care about me," she called out to him as she watched him walk down the hill without her.

"Don't get ahead of yourself." He turned around with a half grin and glanced up at the sky. "You better stay in tonight. There's going to be heavy snow drifts."

She watched as he disappeared into the lodge. She stood for awhile longer looking up into the darkening sky. It was perfectly clear. She twisted her lips, grinning that he'd made one more pitiful attempt to stall her from going out on this date.

•

"It was a wonderful party," an older gentleman told Morgan as she shook his hand with a smile. "We'll see you on Thursday then."

"Thank you," Morgan replied, glancing at the small round clock above the restaurant bar. Ten forty-five. She had made her way to as many people as she could in the past two hours. It gave her enough time to set up meetings with a few possible sponsors, including the overly happy man she'd just left.

He'd been the most important grab of the night. As the CEO for a well-known international magazine, he was friendlier than most other organizational riff-raff.

She'd done her research on him well. He was known to have a weakness for women, and luckily she had all the attributes he liked. She wasn't too keen on using a little provocative persuasion to get what she wanted, but for Vince's sake she was willing to do what she had to, in taste.

With a little bit of cleavage showing at the top of her black dress, and conversations of sunbathing in a bikini on a yacht parked in a baby blue island cove, it had worked like a charm.

Vince was now set up for his first photo shoot.

Morgan sneaked out into the lobby, grabbed her coat off the moose horn coat rack and went outside. Filling her lungs with fresh cold air, a bright red sports car pulled up. It was Max.

"Get in." He opened the door for her from inside the car.

Morgan wanted to tell him she didn't really want to go, but then she wouldn't hear the end of it from him. And as she got inside the car and closed the door, a little voice inside her told her to get back out. It was Vince's voice penetrating her mind.

As they headed down the mountain, she wanted to tell him to turn around and take her back. But he was so excited to have her with him she didn't want to break his heart. After all, she really didn't want to see a grown man cry tonight.

After fifteen minutes of driving around curvy, steep railed drop-offs, she felt a little more at ease. Max was driving slowly, and since he swore he could drive it blindfolded, she relaxed and enjoyed the view.

"Kind of feels like you're flying, huh?" He chuckled as they pulled up to the end of the road and around to a small lookout point.

She nodded as he stopped the car and shifted it into park. An awkward silence passed as they sat there. Max pressed a button above the gear shift and the top hatch began to rise.

Morgan smiled as the top whined back and clicked into place behind them. The frigid air hit her bare legs and she shivered. She could see the stars beautifully.

"Breathtaking, isn't it?" he asked.

"It's beautiful. So, what is this business proposition you have for me?"

He chuckled as he began to tap his fingers on the steering wheel. "Right down to business huh? Well—" He let out a heavy breath through his nose.

It was sudden as he quickly leaned over and pulled her to his lips. He kissed her hard, hurting her as he held her there. Her reaction was complete shock and utter dismay.

"Max," she said in a perturbed voice, trying to push him off her. She tried to break from his grasp, but he wouldn't let her go. His hands wandered under her jacket.

"You know you want me," he said under his erratic breath. "I could sense it from the start."

"Get off!" She tried to move his hands away, but he caught her by the wrists, moving his kiss down to her heaving chest.

She fought him, wiggling in the seat to get him to stop, but he was too overpowering. He pulled her arms up and held her by her wrists with one hand as he used the other to slide up the dress she was wearing.

"Let go of me," she screamed as soon as she felt his hand between her thighs.

Knowing she couldn't avoid hurting him any longer, she raised her knee hard and fast, and planted it in his groin. He let go of her and leaned back in his seat, wincing in pain.

"Damn it," he yelped, leaning over her to open her door. "Get out of my car."

She gladly jumped out onto the cold dark mountain.

"Jerk," she yelled at him. She raised her high heeled right foot and jabbed it into the door, leaving a dark puncture mark in the beautiful red paint.

She watched him speed off, spinning through the trees around the hill and leaving her in the dark. The exasperated breath from her warm mouth fogged the chilled air as she bent down and picked up a small bag that had fallen out with her—cocaine.

She carefully walked to the edge of the cliff near the guard rail trying not to let tears come to her eyes. Unable to see anything except a few lights in the town at the bottom of the mountain, she shivered.

She could see Vince's face now. "I told you so," he said in her mind. It infuriated her into starting the long trek back to the lodge.

After just a few minutes of walking, she began to tremble from the cold. The sounds coming from the trees surrounding her made it worse.

Sticking her hands in her pockets she tried to whistle to keep from losing her nerve. Her lips were beginning to chafe and the only thing that came out was a white puff of fog.

Luckily she had her cell phone in her pocket, but there was nobody to call to come get her. There was no way she was going to call Vince. He'd laugh at her until he was blue in the face, and she wasn't in the mood for that.

"The nerve of him leaving me up here to freeze to death," she scolded through chattering teeth, wishing again she'd listened to Vince's warning. "The creep."

She felt like she'd been walking for hours, but knew it had only been about five minutes. The anger had subsided into fear as the noises around her grew.

Falling snow piles, the footfall of scurrying animals and low growls coming from the hillside finally convinced her it was time to throw in the towel. She had to make the call.

In tears, she pulled her cell phone out of her pocket hoping she had service. There were only a few bars above the service line, but it was enough to get through.

She burst into a nervous shake as she attempted to dial Vince's number. Her fingers trembled as she dialed.

All this time she had refrained from crying over this predicament. She was too strong willed to show fear or even the slightest emotion about what Max had done to her. But when she heard

Vince's deep voice answer the phone, her strength turned into an uncontrollable sob.

"Vince." Morgan's voice cracked as tears streamed her face. Her body shook violently.

"Morgan? What's ... " His voice trailed with static.

"Vince," she yelled, crying loudly. "I need you."

"What happened?" he yelled. "Where are you?"

She sat down on her heels in the middle of the road, wiping at her tears and trying desperately to straighten up long enough to tell him where she was. Then it suddenly dawned on her. She had no idea what directions to give him.

"I don't know where I am," she cried.

"Tell me what you see."

She glanced around. It had started to snow lightly and the only thought she could gather was that she was going to die in the middle of a blizzard. And it'd be her fault for not taking Vince's advice.

"Morgan," he shouted loudly, gathering her attention back to him.

"Um—" She pulled her knees up into her jacket. "Trees. I'm on the other side of the mountain near—" Her voice wavered. "Above the town."

"I'll be right there. Stay put."

She kept the phone to her ear, glancing around her in horror. She heard howls and yelps above and below her in the distance. "Hurry up. I think there are wolves eyeing me as their midnight snack."

"There are no wolves on this mountain."

She heard the sound of his truck in the background and knew he was on his way. It was comforting to know he was still on the line with her, but she couldn't stop crying.

At least her head was warm in the hood of her coat, but she couldn't say the same for her toes. She pushed the bottom of her jacket over them hoping it would help.

By the time she saw the headlights from Vince's truck, her tears were frozen to her face. She couldn't get up from the middle of the road and was glad he had seen her and stopped before he ran her over. It wasn't like he could miss the puffy white snow jacket she was wearing anyway.

He hopped out of his truck and quickly ran to her. He picked her up into his arms and carried her to the passenger side of the truck. He set her down inside, pushing in her jacket and dress so it wouldn't catch in the door.

The heater was on high. She held her frozen hands over the vents as he hopped up inside the truck and put it in gear. She waited for him to give her the "I told you so" speech.

She glanced at him, wondering what was keeping him from saying anything and moving the truck forward. With his eyes wide, he stared at something in the middle of the road before them.

Following his gaze, she leaned forward and glanced over the dash. Two wolves stood in front of the truck, eyes glowing blue in the headlights. They stood still for a brief moment, then scurried across to the hillside where they disappeared into the snow covered brush.

Morgan eyed Vince as he looked at her. His expression was just as shocked as hers. But with the guilt-laden grin he gave her, she knew he'd lied to keep her from worrying.

"I told you they wanted to eat me," she said through chattering teeth.

He chuckled as he drove back up to the lookout where Max had kicked her out. She moaned as he turned them around and headed back down the road.

"I'm such an idiot." She pulled her frozen toes out of her high heels, letting the hot air blow directly on them.

"Why do you say that?" He glanced over at her.

"You were right about him. I should've listened to you." She stared out the side window..

"So what happened?"

Silence filled the cabin of the truck while she thought about it. It felt too strange to tell him Max had almost forced himself on her. Especially considering all the warnings he'd given.

"You don't have to say anything if you don't want to. I have a good idea what happened though."

"You do?"

He glanced at her coolly. "I think Max brought you up here and dropped you off just to get at me." He smirked. "He's done crazy practical jokes before, but this one tops out as his best. He used you, just like I told you he would."

Ah, the "I told you so" speech was in full swing now. She scowled and started to cry again. But this time it wasn't tears of fear or sadness—they were every bit tears of anger.

"You don't know anything about it!"

"I'm right, aren't I?" He watched her tears fall, puzzled by her sudden outburst.

She held her face in her hands and cried as softly as she could.

Glancing up from her swollen eyes, she noticed he had pulled to the side of the road. "Are you kicking me out, too?" She reached over and locked the door. "I don't think so."

"I'm not kicking you out," he said, leaning towards her with his arm stretched across the back of the bench seat. "You're starting to worry me."

She couldn't help crying again. All her life she had chomped at the bit for a good argument and was just plain "tough as an overcooked slice of jerky," her father had always told her. But this time, the urge to sob her way into Vince's arms was too strong.

He held her close, holding his lips to the top of her head as she cried. The warmth of his embrace comforted her enough that she started to tell him what had happened.

"He forced himself on me, the pig."

"Morgan," Vince said, interrupting her. "With your mouth pressed against my coat, I can't hear a word you're saying."

She slowly pulled away from him but kept close enough to keep his arms wrapped around her. "Sorry." She glanced down, afraid to look him in the eyes.

He pulled her chin up gently with his hand, forcing her eyes to his. "Tell me again."

"He—" She sniffled. "He tried to kiss me. When I got out—" She pulled the bag out of her jacket pocket and held it up. "This dropped out."

Vince took it from her hand as she moved back over to her side of the seat. She hadn't wanted to, but she knew if she didn't, she would've stayed there in his arms for the rest of the night.

Sighing, he shook his head in shame. "I knew he was worthless."

She glanced out the window, watching as the snow began to fall fast. Vince was right again as the windy drifts blew at the truck. It seemed he was right about a lot of things.

"Is that all he wanted with you?" he asked, eyeing her curiously.

Afraid of what he might do, she nodded her head in agreement. Pursing her lips, she tried to hide the trembling as more tears began to work in her eyes. It wasn't because she was almost forced into having sex with someone she now despised, but the fact she had trusted someone she barely knew and was betrayed.

"How'd that get torn?" He pointed out the rip along the neckline of her dress.

She hadn't noticed it. Glancing down at the rip in the stretched out neckline, she faked her knowledge of it.

"I covered up my face with it when I was waiting for you. It must have happened then."

An irritated breath escaped his lips as he shifted the truck into gear and started the drive back towards the lodge. He obviously didn't believe her.

"If he tried to—" His voice trailed. "I'll kill him."

A quiet solitude crept over the rumbling of the engine as she stared out the window. The heavy snow panned into the brightness of the headlights, and then faded as it fell below the hood of the truck.

The road was covered with a white blanket, but she felt safe being there with Vince. It was warm and comfortable, not at all like the nervous feeling she had when she got in Max's car.

It was past midnight by the time they finally pulled into the parking lot at the lodge. Her tears had come and gone and then come again every time she thought about what happened.

She was afraid to stay in Vince's company any longer, afraid he might bring it back up and work the truth out of her. She quickly unlocked the door and started for the handle.

"Wait," he said.

She didn't listen. She hopped out of the truck and briskly walked across the lot to the lobby entrance ignoring his comment that she was the most stubborn woman he'd ever known.

But the truth was, she couldn't wait to get to her room, take a hot shower and snuggle up under the warm wool blankets on her bed. It had been too long of a night to worry any more about it. And as far as she knew, the entire night was nothing more than a bad dream.

Chapter 7

She slept in until noon and would've slept longer if it wasn't for the loud bang of someone knocking at her door. Groggily, she rose out of bed and opened it to Vince's grinning face as he held out a piece of paper to her.

"I found this outside your door," he said.

Sighing heavily, she grabbed the paper out of his hand. It was from Max, apologizing about last night. She wadded it up, tossed it onto the floor and got back in bed, pulling the blanket over her head.

Vince walked into the room and closed the door behind him. "We have a busy day today."

"It's Sunday," Morgan mumbled, pressing her face against the covers. "Go away."

He sat down at the edge of the bed and bounced a few times. "Come on. Get up and get your clothes on. I'm taking you out."

She pulled the blanket down below her chin and glared at him. "Where are we going?" she asked unenthused.

He smiled. "You, my dear, are going to learn how to ski."

"I don't want to." She covered her face back up, wishing he would leave her alone.

"Yes, you do." He pulled the cover back down and chuckled at her hair that had fluffed into her face. "I'm not leaving until you're up."

Obviously he wasn't going to give up as he consistently

bounced on the bed. The rustle of his snowsuit was enough to make her wince in aggravation.

"Okay, okay." She shuffled into the bathroom and closed the door.

Smiling, Vince lay back on the bed and waited with a smirk. He was good, too good at making someone do what he wanted, although it didn't take too much convincing for her.

"I was planning on going into the city this week," Morgan called from the bathroom door as she brushed her teeth and spit in the sink. "You have a photo shoot on Thursday anyway, so maybe we can ride in together."

"With who?"

"The ski magazine that picked you up last night," Morgan said proudly.

"Yeah, okay. My parents invited us to dinner anyway."

He didn't put in much thought to his answer, as his attention was on the wadded piece of paper in the floor. Fighting the urge to pick it up, he lay back on the bed, propping himself up with his elbow.

He glanced around the room. There were clothes in the floor. There were more strung over the brown recliner in the corner of the room, including her undergarments, which struck a spark in his eyes.

Morgan came out of the bathroom with a refreshing smile. She pulled her light blue snowsuit out of the large oak dresser that was also covered in clothes.

"Don't take this wrong, but you're a slob," he said playfully.

She scowled at him and grabbed a towel from the linen closet beside the bathroom door. "Thanks. I appreciate your observation."

"The day will be over by the time you're finished getting ready."

He lay back on the bed, folding his hands behind his head.

Morgan went into the bathroom and started the shower. "Why am I going anywhere with him?" she whispered. "This is supposed to be my day off."

Her stomach growled as she washed her hair. She knew she had to get something to eat before they took the trek up the mountain.

She had never wanted to learn to ski, although her father had tried to take her more than once. They would get to the lodge, but it always ended up as a winter fishing trip instead.

Vince waited at the edge of the bed, eyeing the wrinkled ball of paper in the floor, trying desperately to keep from picking it up and reading it. But with Morgan in the shower, she would never know.

He reached down, picked it up and quickly read it. Hearing the shower turn off, he wadded it back up and put it back where it was. The anger in him rose. He felt like going ballistic at the thought of her being left out on the mountain to freeze to death.

Morgan stepped out of the bathroom drying her hair with the towel. She found her dryer under the small pile of clothes on the dresser and plugged it into the outlet.

He paced the room watching her as she dried her hair. The aroma of the flower scented shampoo she used made him breathe deeply.

"You smell good," he said as soon as she finished.

She grinned. "Thanks. It's this new shampoo I'm using."

"It suits you," he replied, leaning back on the door.

When they finally stepped out of her room and made their way down the winding staircase to the lobby.

"I'm starving." Morgan stopped at the doorway to the restaurant and leaned inside.

He sighed impatiently. "What do you want?"

"Anything, as long as it's edible," she answered unzipping her coat.

"Just stay here. I'll get you something." He went into the restaurant quickly and came back with a biscuit smothered in butter and jelly on a napkin.

Morgan glanced at the messy morsel and frowned. "You expect me to eat that?"

"It's a biscuit. It's edible and it'll tide you over until we get to the top of the lift."

"Lift?" she asked nervously. "I'm not going on a lift."

"Yes, you are." He vivaciously flashed his teeth.

"It's a height thing," she growled.

"You're stubborn woman."

"It takes a stubborn man to notice."

Taking the biscuit from his hand, she commenced eating it. She wasn't going to admit it was delicious as she finished it off. She could've eaten scrambled eggs and bacon with it, but he was rearing to get going, rather impatiently.

"Come on."

"You know," she said as he took her by the hand and led her out the side entrance of the lobby, "patience is a virtue."

She trekked up beside him, wondering where he was taking her until they reached a small shop lined with skis. She followed him inside and ogled at all the ski equipment.

"Vince." A gray haired man, dressed with a large grin stood with admiration. "I haven't seen you in here in a while."

"Hey, George." Vince smiled back, pulling Morgan up to the counter with him.

"We were so busy here yesterday." George went on as he made change for a paying customer. "Thank you ma'am," he told her as she grabbed the rented skis and left with a quick smile at Vince.

Morgan propped her elbows on the counter, admiring the bracelets in the glass case near the cash register. They were pure silver and each one had a name etched into it. She looked for her name, but disappointedly didn't find it.

"They never have my name," she whined.

Vince glanced down at what she was looking at. He rolled his eyes when he saw what she was talking about, then returned his attention to George.

"So what can I do for you?" George went on, rubbing his bearded chin with a squint to his eye.

Vince cleared his throat. "Need a one in Shape skis and boots."

George smiled and turned around to the selection of skis on

the wall. "Teaching today, huh?"

"You could say that." Vince nodded, glancing at Morgan who was now looking at a collection of colored wrist bands.

"What size boots do you need?" George asked moving a small step stool to reach the shelf above him.

Vince looked down at her feet. "Uh, a nine?"

She peered at him beneath lowered brows. "Seven and a half."

"All I have is an eight." George climbed the stool and grabbed a pair of black boots. "Make sure they're not too loose or you're feet will be killing you by the time you're done."

Vince handed the skis to her outside. She fumbled to keep hold of them as he put his hands on her shoulders and looked her straight in the eyes.

"Listen, I don't want you to get mad at me when you find out where I'm taking you." His voice was serious. "It's not to offend your—" From the corner of his eye, he watched as a ski fell from her grasp and landed in the snow. He tried to ignore the interruption as he finished his sentence. "—skills."

Morgan, although curious, was about to give up on learning to ski already, but obviously he wasn't going to let her. He picked up the fallen, sunken-in-snow ski and took her by the hand. With a quick step, he guided her to the lift.

It looked scary. Hands-down, flat-out, undeniably frightening. There was no way she was going to ride that thing straight up the mountain without being knocked out first.

With a quick glance to Vince, she could tell he knew how she was feeling. He tried to reassure her with a sweet smile as he led her to a bench and helped her put on her skis.

"It'll be fine." He stood up and pulled her to her feet. He held on to her elbow and guided her to the lift area. "Just watch the bench as it comes towards you and hop on. It's that easy."

She felt like closing her eyes and passing out from the tension, but she kept them glued on the chair that was coming for them. Her heart raced.

Holding her breath, she fell back on it and sat down. Holding tight to Vince's arm, they ascended into the air swinging back and forth. She squealed in horrified delight as she left her heart on the ground.

"Open your eyes," he said, elbowing her playfully. "It's beautiful."

She opened one eye, peeking, but was too afraid to look around. She kept her attention on his grinning face as he gazed around at the scenery.

Slowly, she found the courage to turn her head and look out at the mountain. It was breathtaking. The exhilaration she felt from the view left her head spinning. Somehow, she thought maybe the ride would be like a roller coaster, as silly as that was, but it was relaxing, serene and best of all—real.

Everything was white. From the marvelous slant beneath them to the tips of the trees, winter had spread itself out marvelously. The frigid air hit her nose and cheeks, but the warmth of the moment let her happily accept it. She didn't want it to end, but could see it coming as they neared another log building above them.

"This is the tricky part," Vince said, startling her thoughts.

"What do you mean?" she asked, swallowing the lump in her throat at what was coming up.

"Well," he chuckled, "you're about to get a crash course in skiing. Hopefully no pun is intended in what I just said."

"I don't understand."

"Technically this part of the lift is for people who can already ski. It'll let you off on a slope in some places to give you a small boost."

"What?" She gasped.

"Don't worry. It's just the beginners and cross-country area. The slope's not that steep."

"I can't believe this." Her heart skipped. "I can barely walk in these things. How do you expect me to ski in them?"

"Just hang on to me when we get off. I won't let you fall."

She eyed the flat area coming up, feeling the lump in her throat broaden. Her grip tightened around his arm as the time came to hop off.

He pulled her out of the bench and she went flying down the small slope. He let her go and stopped in the middle of the hill, eagerly watching her.

"You can stop now," he yelled at her.

"I don't know how," she yelled back, holding tight to the poles as the middle of the hill turned into a new slope, one much steeper than the first.

Her hands flew up into the air. She dropped her poles on the ground and began to lose her balance. The scream she let out attracted a few stares, including one shocked glance from Vince who finally caught up to her and offered her his hand. She grabbed tight and held on for dear life.

"Hang on," he yelled over the shushing noise of the skis.

He turned her towards a small wall of snow built on an incline. She breathed a sigh of relief as they finally slowed down, but unfortunately it wasn't enough.

Holding her breath and closing her eyes, she blocked out the noise. Finding silence within the moment, she tried desperately not to believe it was coming, but there was no use for faith now.

In an instant, they both hit the wall. Her eyes opened wide with fear as she gripped his hand tightly. She fell forward in the snow and landed on the ground, pulling him down with her on his backside.

As they slid down the wall, the thought of going over the embankment and falling further down the hill kept fear from leaving her eyes. With her mouth agape, she finally came to a full stop by slamming her body into Vince's legs.

As she lay on her stomach, she stared up at him with a horrified expression on her face. With mouth open and eyes widened, she found her hands around Vince's legs and her head between his thighs. She let out a terrified gasp as she scrambled to turn over and get away from the compromising position as he began to laugh.

Angry he was finding humor in the moment, she punched him in the leg. "It's not funny."

"You should've seen yourself." He genuinely laughed, shaking his head in shear enjoyment.

Her aggravated tension quickly melted when he continued laughing, loudly, as he sat in the snow beside her almost in tears. She spit snow from her mouth as she, too, began to laugh.

"You said you wouldn't let me fall." She cupped a handful of snow and tossed it at him playfully. "My butt is freezing. Help me up."

He rose to his feet, still laughing as he held his hands out for her to take. "Come on."

She gladly accepted and he pulled her up to her feet. "I lost my poles."

"We'll pick them up on the way."

"Where are you taking me anyway?" she asked curiously, trying to keep her balance as he helped her get back up the slope.

"You'll see. I fill in once a month for the guy who runs the show."

He led her behind another ski shop to a small and flat snowy meadow with young falling kids. Awing as a boy with skis propped over his shoulder ran up to Vince, she realized it was a class.

"Mr. Evans is here," he yelled and turned back to a group of kids sitting on their rear ends smiling and shouting out hellos with an enthusiastic wave.

"Hey guys," Vince said, kneeling down to the boy who had the biggest smile on his face.

Morgan tossed a confused but intrigued glance as he walked over to the now lined-up kids. She had no idea he taught a kids' class. It was a refreshing light to see him in.

"How are you?" Vince asked them, slapping fives to a few of the boys and poking the noses of the giggling over-stuffed, pink-suited girls.

"Fine," they all said in unison.

"Today, we have a special guest," he said, pacing the line of smiling kids with a grin. He waved Morgan over to him. "I want you all to say hi to my special friend, Morgan."

"Hi, Morgan," all seven said in slow harmony.

"Hi there." She greeted them warmly with a grin as she threw Vince a puzzled glance.

"Ms. Price is going to join our class today." He shrugged with a sweet smile. "You guys are much better at skiing than she is."

The kids laughed, tumbling down to the ground and embarrassing her completely. With flushed cheeks, she puffed out her lips playfully.

"Corey." He pulled a short blond boy from the line as the kids quieted down. "I want you to lead the team in booting up today."

"Okay." Corey clenched his fist and jerked his elbow in, and with an excited voice said, "Yes."

Morgan was nicely ordered to stand with the line of kids in front of Corey. He instructed them on how to loop laces with an obvious memorized line while showing them at the same time how to walk in their boots.

"When you walk without your skis, walk on your heels," he said bashfully.

Vince watched behind Morgan. He snickered when Corey corrected her.

"Hey. Don't laugh at me. I'm new at this."

Vince took over the class and taught them how to balance. His presentation of showing what would happen if balance was lost by falling back in the snow left the kids rolling on the ground in hyperactive laughter. She found herself laughing with them.

Although she felt a little odd being in a children's class, she actually had fun. And by the time the class was over, she'd even learned a few things about skiing.

As each child was picked up by their parents, they shook Vince's hand with a smile. She watched him talk with several of them, raving over how good of a skier their child was going to be.

Some of the kids hugged him before they left, and although she'd never really been around children much, she thought it was the cutest thing she'd ever seen.

And as the last kid from the class finally walked away, he sat down beside her in the snow with a relieved sigh. He turned to her with a large, innocent grin.

"So, why didn't you tell me about this before?" she asked, bumping her elbow into his.

"You never gave me a chance," he replied. He stared at her as if memorizing her face. "I'd like to spend more time with you on a personal level though. Then you might change your mind about me. I'm really not that big of a jerk."

She felt like melting. The way his eyes shone green as he gazed into hers made her heart pound. He was beautiful. Every shred of will she had fought the urge to throw her body at his feet and beg for him to take her to her room and make mad love to her.

"So how did I do on my first lesson?" she asked, trying to ignore the naked images of him that flashed through her mind.

"Well, let's see." He stood up and held his hands out to her. She gracefully accepted, and he pulled her up to her feet.

"Your balance is a bit off." He turned her around and stood behind her. "You're putting too much weight on your toes." Pulling her back by her shoulders, he leaned her against him. He lowered his lips close to her ear, and whispered. "This is how you should do it."

She shivered at his touch, enjoying the sensation pouring through her body as he pulled her feet up onto his and stepped with her. His hands squeezed her arms gently, sensually, with every step they took until they stopped behind the building.

He moved his lips down to her earlobe, nuzzling lightly. His warm breath on her neck made her skin rise. She closed her eyes and swallowed hard.

"I think I got it," she finally said as she managed to break free from his grasp and quickly move away with a nervous laugh. "Thanks for the lesson."

He gave her an apprehensive glance. "Why are you running away from me?"

"I'm not running away."

For a long time they stared at each other. She shifted her weight, biting her lower lip nervously until finally he sighed.

"I give up," he said, realizing she wasn't going to give him a good enough answer.

He shook his head and started back towards the lift, leaving her standing there feeling like a schmuck. She quickly picked up her skis from the ground and went after him.

"Wait," she yelled, balancing the toppling skis around her as she tromped through the snow, and finally resorted to dragging them behind her like a sled.

"I'm tired of waiting for you," he said angrily turning around to face her. His brows lowered, but it wasn't the playfully hateful glare he usually gave her when they argued. He was genuinely mad at her.

Tired of dealing with the uncooperative skis, she dropped them in the snow behind her. "Why are you so upset?"

"I don't know Morgan. You tell me."

"Was I doing something wrong?"

"Everything is always wrong, isn't it?"

He walked back up to her, bent down and picked up the skis with a huff. He put them together and balanced them on his shoulder.

"Nothing's wrong. I just didn't feel comfortable being that close." She lied—and *completely* through her teeth.

"Do you think I'm trying to get you in bed? Because that's the way you're acting." He turned away and started back up the hill towards the lift.

Morgan watched in frustration, unsure of what to say. "No," she said aloud, following him. "You just read too much into it. I've already told you I'm not interested in anything but business."

He turned around quickly. "You're the most stubborn, downright ignorant woman I've ever met. I was giving you a lesson, that's all it was."

She stood appalled as he sat down in the lift bench and waved goodbye to her with a large aggravated grin. He was leaving her there with no skis.

Anger, irritation and enough steam that the snow could suddenly melt all around her, billowed from every pore of her body.

The fear of riding the lift sank deep in her mind as she turned her backside to the bench two chairs behind him.

She hopped on, not caring she wasn't wearing skis for the dismount. The ride was so slow it would be easy to run off when she landed anyway. Hopefully there was no hill this time.

She watched the back of Vince's head on the way down.

It wasn't so bad. At least she didn't turn into a runaway skier as she stepped off the bench and followed Vince towards the lodge. When she walked into the lobby, a small crowd had gathered around in a group near the front desk. Curious, she walked over to see what was going on.

Max was signing autographs with a half-cocked grin. She tried to duck out and leave before he saw her, but it was too late. He'd already made eye contact.

"Morgan." A smile lingered in his eyes and the other half of his grin appeared.

She rolled her eyes, ignoring his efforts to stop her as she stormed off to her room. She didn't want anything to do with anyone, especially him.

She shut the door to her room and leaned back against it. The nerve of him, getting angry when she did nothing but move away from his strong, muscular arms that had held her so delicately, beautifully, sensually.

She closed her eyes, thinking about it, wanting it and longing for it again. She'd stay in them this time if she could.

Shaking it off, she scolded herself for thinking that way about him. It had to stay professional. *Business only for him,* she thought as she pulled off the boots.

With a sigh that the day had not worked out as well as she hoped, she plopped herself down on the bed. Glancing at the boots with a puckered brow, she realized she'd forgotten to take them back to the rental shop.

Chapter 8

"We were expecting you yesterday." Emma greeted Vince and Morgan at the front door of their house. She led them inside where Ed and Chad were sitting in the living room watching a football game blaring on their widescreen TV that stretched over half the wall.

"Yeah, what happened?" Chad said tossing a football up in the air and catching it without looking up from the television.

"We were caught up in traffic, bro." Vince smirked, taking off his jacket and joining them.

Emma led Morgan into the kitchen. "How have you been?"

"Wonderful." Morgan felt warmth in her cheeks when she answered. "How are you?"

"Oh." Emma pulled out a large pot from one of the white floor cabinets and set it on the stove. "Besides the fact our cook is taking the day off to get his hair done and I'm the designated chef today, I'm doing just fine." She smiled sweetly. "I'm not much of a cook."

Her raspy laugh echoed through the kitchen.

"Anything I can help you with?" Morgan asked, sliding her jacket off her arms and draping it over a high back stool near the breakfast bar.

"I'm planning on a pot roast and salad for dinner. Would you be a dear and cut up some vegetables?"

Morgan opened the refrigerator and pulled out a variety of

ingredients to make a Caesar salad and carried them to the sink. Emma had everything ready for her from the cutting board to the colander.

As Morgan chopped a juicy head of romaine lettuce, she watched Vince through the gap between the counter and overhead cabinets. He was so different than how he was when they first met, talking and laughing with his family.

Although she felt a little awkward being there with them like she were part of their family, it felt good. She felt like she belonged and a smile draped across her face.

Her heart leapt when she caught Vince's eyes from time to time as she shredded carrots, chopped onions and tomatoes. She even peeled potatoes for Emma's roast, which already smelled delicious as she seared it.

"You're glowing," Emma whispered, staring at her with a smile as she leaned against the counter next to her. "Something happened between you two, didn't it?"

"No." Morgan shook her head. "He's just mad at me."

"Now what could he possibly be mad at you about?" she asked with a stern gaze.

"It's nothing." Morgan grinned as she thought about that moment he held her in his arms.

She didn't want anyone to know she had feelings for Vince, but she should've known Emma would see right through her. After all, a woman at her age probably went through the same exact things as she had before she met the right man.

Emma gasped in excitement. "You're in love with him."

Morgan put her finger to her lips shushing Emma's excited squeal. Trying to hold back her laughter, she fixed her eyes rigidly on hers. "I am not."

"I know love when I see it." Emma pulled all the peels and unusable cuts from the colander and tossed them in the garbage under the sink. "I knew you both would end up together after the first time you met."

"We're not together." Morgan glanced at her curiously as she tossed the scrumptious salad with two wooden forks she found hanging from a utensil hook.

"I know my son. He's not the perfect gentleman to say the least." Emma scowled slightly at him as he watched the game. "He wears his father's frown most of the time, which leads me to believe there is something there when it comes to you."

"Oh, he's just happy because his team is winning." Morgan snickered as she found the plastic wrap in the drawer beside the refrigerator.

Emma took the plastic wrap from her hands, set it down on the counter and took hold of her shoulders. She turned her around and walked her back to the counter, facing the living room.

"I know you're confused, but that right there should sum everything I just said up nicely." She gave a quick point with her thumb at Vince.

Morgan watched as the three men cheered when their team scored a touchdown. But it wasn't until they settled back into their seats did she notice what Emma was talking about.

As Ed and Chad went back to zombie blank stares at the television, Vince continued to genuinely smile. It grew bigger when he caught her staring at him, and she suddenly blushed.

Turning away quickly, her heart pounded in her chest, leaping to her throat with a nervous desire to run around screaming in excitement. But whether she liked it or not, she had to fight it, deny it, or do something to keep it from overwhelming her.

"Come on, dear." Emma said as she closed the oven door on her roast. "I want to show you something."

Morgan followed her through the living room. She smiled as Vince watched them walk behind the couch towards the hallway. He looked worried.

Emma led her to the end of the hall and into a beautiful sunken in den. "A red room," Morgan said as Emma sat down on a white leather couch.

"Ed hates this room. He says the color makes him feel angry." She laughed. "The old fool has always been a grouch."

Morgan sat down beside her and watched her open the old wooden chest that doubled as a coffee table. Inside were photo albums, many that had obviously been collected over the years by the fragile look of their covers.

"I swore I would never be able to do this with any of my boys. I never thought they'd bring home a girl worthy to show these to."

Morgan grinned as she opened one of the photo albums. A small version of Vince stood smiling in a pair of bell-bottom jeans. His hair matched the black shirt he wore as he held a snowboard up for the person taking the picture.

Emma stood up. "You go ahead and look through what you want. I'll be back in a few minutes."

"Thanks," Morgan said as she watched her leave the room.

She returned her attention to the photos and thumbed through them. There were so many pictures of Vince on his snowboard. Some were also taken with a trophy in hand and a smile across his young sweet face. There were first place ribbons stuck between the pages from competitions he'd won as a child.

It was easy to see how dedicated he was to the sport. Not one picture of him in the entire album was taken without snow at his feet or a snowboard or skis in his hands.

"Uh oh," Vince said as he walked into the room, smiling slyly.

Morgan glanced at him with a grin as he sat down beside her on the couch. His face seemed to glow in embarrassment that his mother had gotten out the family photos.

"I can't believe she's letting you look at these." He twisted his lips as he looked down at one of the photos and chuckled. "That one's taken on Mt. Hood in Portland. I was fifteen when I competed there."

"Did you win?"

"Nah. I came in second out of fifty kids that weekend."

"That's still pretty good," she said smiling at him.

A moment of silence passed. As she stared at his pictures, a tender emotion hit her hard. She blushed.

"Listen," she said, "I'm sorry about Sunday."

"I'm over it." Vince raised his hand and yanked a lock of her hair playfully. "You're beautiful," he whispered as he leaned in to steal a light kiss.

The kiss sent sudden chills throughout her body, making her tremble slightly. He cupped her face in his hands and pulled her against him as the kiss deepened.

Fear of falling into his arms and letting him take her away into passion made her break away from his grasp. She sat back, trying desperately not to work her way back over to him. By the glance on his face, she could tell he was irritated with her, yet again.

"Your mother might come in," she said as she got up from the couch.

"Wait a second," he said following her to the doorway and catching her before she could make her getaway. "It was just a kiss."

She loved the way he stroked her hair away from her neck. The melting sensation inside her made her close her eyes and enjoy it, knowing she shouldn't allow him that close. But she couldn't help it, not this time.

She quickly balanced on her tip-toes and threw her arms around his neck. Planting her lips on his, she opened her mouth and kissed him. But the longing for him ended abruptly when his mother walked into the room.

"Dinner's about ready you two."

Emma caught Morgan's guilty eyes and smiled. And before she left the room she mouthed the words, "I told you so."

•

Chad leaned over the dinner table and kissed Emma on the cheek with a loud smack and sat back down in his chair, completely full. "You're amazing as always, Mother. That was delicious."

Emma grinned, turning her soft white skin into a shade of pink. "You're so right."

"Salads are for goats, but it was good," Chad added, smiling at Morgan who sat next to Emma.

Vince sat across from Morgan, meeting her eyes a few times during the meal. She was seeing him differently now. After finally returning his kiss without a fight, it seemed his smile never left him, and she proudly took it in.

"Despite the good dinner—" Ed laid his fork down on his empty plate with a sigh that he was full. "I'm more interested in what's for dessert."

Emma smacked him playfully on the arm. "Desserts are Lance's specialty, not mine. I didn't make one."

"Lance?" Morgan asked with a puzzled look. Vince and Chad both chuckled at the mention of his name.

Emma shushed them with a growl. "I hired Lance to be our cook. He needed a job while he goes to culinary school, so I gave him one." She paused for a moment. "He swings the other way if you catch my meaning."

"He makes us fig pies in a pink tutu," Ed said in a serious tone, moaning at his overstuffed stomach.

Vince and Chad burst out into laughter at their father's comment. It was almost too much to watch them laugh hysterically when Morgan tried desperately to hold in her own.

Emma didn't laugh. She scolded each of them for not respecting Lance's individuality. "Just because he likes to dress in tutus and halter tops doesn't mean he's not part of our family."

She tried diligently to make it into a serious conversation. But she only made it worse by putting more comical images in their heads.

"I'm ashamed at all of you." Emma let out a snort and began to laugh. "He is your cousin, you know."

She stood up with a huff and began clearing the dirty dishes.

Morgan stood up and picked up her plate. "Let me clean up. You've done so much already," she told Emma.

"No, dear, you go on and sit down."

Vince stood up and began to help. "Go to the couch, Mom. We got this."

With a smile, Emma agreed to let them take over. "Thank you."

As Morgan rinsed each dish and added it to the pile already in the dishwasher, she watched Vince. He'd clear another few dishes from the table and bring them to her, sneaking in a kiss on her cheek every time he set one in the sink. And when the last dish was finally finished, he grabbed their jackets and pulled her out the front door into the cold night air.

As if he hadn't seen her in weeks, he grabbed her, pulled her into his arms and kissed her. Closing her eyes, she enjoyed his touch as he caressed her back and pulled her body close to his.

When he broke away from her lips, he smiled. "I've been dying to kiss you like that all night."

She breathed heavily. The excitement rushing through her body was unbelievable. She ached for more of his tender kiss and the gentle touch of his hands.

He placed his hand in hers and raised it to his lips. He kissed her fingers one by one until each one of them were tingling. Kissing the back of her hand as if she were a princess, he began to lead her down the driveway and around to the back of the house.

"I hope you don't mind taking a walk in the cold," he said as he tucked her arm under his. "I thought it might be nice to spend a little time alone."

"It's a beautiful night," she said shivering slightly as they walked through the gate to the pool.

"It just seems like yesterday when we met here," he said.

"Three months," she said. "You hated me then."

"I didn't hate you," he replied with a look of dismay. "Actually, I thought you were the most beautiful woman I'd ever seen." He stopped her at the fountain that had been turned off for the winter and pulled her against him. "You still are."

She eyed him closely. The way he was talking to her was just too strange to believe. Something was definitely up.

"What's really going on here?" she asked as she gazed up into his eyes. "Why are you being so nice?"

"What?" he shrugged with a puzzled glance. "You want me to be mean to you?"

"It'd be more believable," she replied.

"Wow," he remarked as he pulled from their embrace and folded his arms over his chest. He stared at her wide-eyed. "You're incredible."

The air around them suddenly grew quiet. Tension worked

up inside her as he stared at her without a twitch of his straight lipped face, or a change of his stance.

"Why are you staring at me like that?" she finally asked, breaking the silence.

"Like what?" he asked, barely blinking.

"Like that."

"I'm waiting for you to figure it out," he growled.

"Figure what out?"

"That you're as stubborn as a mule. You can't even take a compliment without thinking there are ulterior motives." He sighed.

"I don't think you have ulterior motives," she said. "I just think you're being nice to me for a specific reason. I'm just curious as to why."

"Can't you just stop analyzing everything I do or say to you?" He grabbed her arms and gently squeezed. "I wanted to kiss you, so I did. I brought you out here because I wanted to show you—" He reached into his pocket and pulled out an envelope. "I wanted to show you this."

"What is it?"

"I got this in the mail on Monday." He handed it to her to read.

The header had an official Olympic seal. She glanced up at him with a sudden grin as she pulled out the letter and unfolded it. It was an acceptance letter as a qualifier for the American team. She suddenly grew excited.

"Why didn't you tell me about this before?"

"You were mad at me."

"No, you were mad at me."

"It doesn't matter," he said ending the argument before it got started. "Besides, I didn't know what to say to thank you for the work you put into this." He grinned when she returned with a smile.

"You don't owe me anything."

"I've been wrong about you from the beginning," he added, taking her by the hand and pulling her close to him. "I thought you were going to be like all the rest of them. But you—" He kissed her lightly on the lips. "You really are doing this for me."

She gave a quaint smile. "I love seeing someone with talent become the person they want to be." She hesitantly swiped a dark lock from his eye. "You're going to qualify. There's no doubt in my mind."

He smiled, stroking her cheek with the back of his hand. "You're the best thing that's happened to my career."

Morgan blushed again. None of her clients had ever said anything like that to her. No matter how much she worked to get them into the sweet spot of their career, they'd never said anything to her but a quick thank you.

Tears swelled in her eyes. She tried to hide them but one escaped and ran down her cheek.

He wiped it with his thumb. "I didn't mean to make you cry."

"I'm just happy for you. And I'm sorry."

"For what?" he asked.

"For giving you a hard time," she replied.

He laughed. It was the deep raspy voice she loved to hear from him. It sent chills through her, the kind she loved to feel, the kind that intoxicated her, making her want to fall into his arms. And that was exactly what she did.

Before she could stop it from happening, she wrapped her arms around his torso and leaned against him. She felt his arms around her shoulders and his lips press against the top of her head.

She closed her eyes as they swayed together. Holding him for what seemed the longest moment, a wonderful moment, she didn't want to let go.

"We should go," he said, pushing her back to meet his glance. "It's getting late and we have a big day tomorrow."

She nodded. "I need to get home to see how many more plants of mine have died by Sally's black thumb."

He threw her a pleasant grin. As he took her hand in his and led her back down the path toward the house, she sighed.

Although the moment was real and the timing was right, for some reason, she couldn't shake that letting her feelings go was a big mistake. And just as she was about to invite him to come home with her for the night, she closed her mouth and didn't say a word.

Chapter 9

The backdrop behind Vince was amazing. A mural of snow-peaked mountains lined a backlit screen. Bright studio lights hung from the ceiling, giving it a three-dimensional effect.

There were only a few people there during the shoot, which made it less tense for Vince. It was obvious for Morgan to see he was nervous. She had seen even the most famous people clam up with sweat, constantly keeping the makeup artist on their toes.

He looked handsome in his black long-sleeve shirt that fit tight around his chest. And his blue jeans—there wasn't a pair he didn't look good in.

He cooperated with the constant flash of the camera and the directions given by the photographer as he moved him around into various positions. One in which Morgan found completely irresistible as he looked down at the floor with a grin that could make a woman fall to her knees. She wanted that photo for herself, though she wasn't sure how she'd explain it to anyone that caught her with it.

One of the representatives from the magazine shook his hand, thanking him for coming in. He let him know they were coming up to the lodge in a few days to get live action shots and an interview, which made Vince give Morgan a nervous glance.

With a relieved sigh, he finally walked out of the studio with Morgan striding along next to him. He was glad it was over as he wiped a bead of sweat from his brow.

"You did great." She walked beside him up the ramp that led to the parking garage elevator.

"I just hope I don't bite during the live shots." He laughed holding the glass door open for her. "I'm surprised you didn't tell me they were coming up to the lodge."

"I told you about it. You just weren't listening."

They walked inside the small paved lobby where the elevators were. Tires squealed above them from leaving cars circling down the exit ramp to the street. It gave her the feeling she was truly home.

"How did your plants look last night when you got home?" he asked as they stepped inside the elevator.

"I was too tired to check."

"Sally has a black thumb, huh?" he asked as the doors closed.

"She's supposed to be watering them at least twice a week, but she's been so busy planning her wedding she's let a few die already." She twisted her lips. "I'm sure the plant cemetery beside my house has grown."

"We can stop there before we head out of town if you like."

"You don't mind?"

"No." He palmed her back as the doors opened, and walked beside her to the truck.

In all the dates she'd ever been on, he was the first who had ever opened the door for her. Not saying this was a date, but it sent a grin across her face.

As they drove down the street, Vince flipped the radio on and smiled at the old nineties grunge song. He turned it up slightly.

"I haven't heard this song in years."

Morgan grinned, remembering the time when the song was popular on the radio. "I was at a party when I first heard this one," she said, smiling out the window at the memories. "My friend's parents went out of town one weekend and we invited everyone we knew over. They came home in the middle of the party to find their house completely covered in toilet paper."

"Sounds like a typical teenage night."

Morgan laughed. "Yeah, it was a lot of fun."

"The same thing happened to me one night," he said, merging into traffic on the four-lane highway. "I think it was mandatory for kids back then to get caught at least once before they graduated from high school."

She agreed with a nod. "I can imagine your parents throwing a fit."

"You have no idea how my mother can get." He threw her a relaxed grin. "She's like a she-devil with red glowing eyes who watches you even when she's not there."

Realizing they were about to miss the exit, she pointed in a panic. "Get off here!"

He slammed on his brakes and squealed the tires through the white lines, cutting off to the ramp just before the concrete shoulder. She held on tight, fearing they were going to wreck, cringing as a car fell into place behind them and laid in thick on the horn.

He pulled the truck around the sharp curve leading to the highway laughing. Glancing in the rear-view mirror, he made sure the other car was okay.

"We're good," he said grinning mischievously.

"More like crazy," she announced, afraid to let go of the bar above the truck door.

"If you would've told me before we got there, that wouldn't have happened."

"Well, if you'd slow down a little, I could tell you in time."

"I'm not speeding."

"Yes you were. You were going sixty-five in a fifty-five zone."

"I was going sixty at the most."

"Sixty-five," she corrected him again.

With a chuckling growl, he gave up. "You're too much, you know that?"

"Turn left at the next light."

She grinned playfully, knowing the intersection was at least another mile away. She glanced out the window, believing she was starting to like their little arguments.

It was a sight for sore eyes. The familiar path of houses seemed to wave as they neared her home. A smile escaped her tired lips as she dug into her purse for the keys to the front door.

She jumped out of the truck and ran up the porch steps before he could turn off the engine. Unlocking the door, she noticed one of her plants outside was missing. *Black thumb Sally*, she thought as she walked inside to the foyer.

"Nice place," Vince said looking around as he shut the door behind him. He watched Morgan move from room to room looking at her half-dead plants and moaning in disappointment at each one.

"I have got to hire someone who knows how to take care of plants."

She picked up one of her jade trees. Noticing a few brown spots on it, she groaned.

Vince wandered around, picking up pictures. Most of the photographs were of Morgan posing with friends. He picked up one of her and an older gray-haired gentleman posing at a baseball stadium with their arms around each other.

"Who's this?" he asked her as she ran a pitcher of water in the kitchen.

She turned the water off and walked over to him. "Oh, that's my dad."

He nodded as he looked at a younger Morgan with jeans, a T-shirt and NY Yankee ball cap on. "I thought you weren't into sports."

"I'm not." She walked around to her plants and soaked the dry soil in their pots. "My dad was a Yankees fan, so I went with him to a few of the games. He got me the hat I'm wearing in the picture from one of the players."

"Oh, which one did he get it from?"

"I really don't know," she said, finger to mouth and then returned to her dying plants.

"Where do your parents live?" he asked, realizing he'd never heard her talk about them.

"Well." She sighed. "My mom died when I was only two. And my dad passed away about seven years ago in a car accident."

He sank down into the cushions of the tan sectional couch in the living room and his heart went right along with it. "I'm sorry to hear that."

"It's fine. It was a long time ago," she said and set the pitcher down in the sink. "The remote is in front of you if you'd like to watch TV."

He grabbed it off the glass coffee table and turned the television on. Flipping through channels, he stopped on a football game. It was third quarter and Minnesota was down a touchdown from Kansas.

"Typical." Morgan grinned watching him from the kitchen.

He shrugged. "You have your plants to water."

Ignoring his comment, she went out onto her back patio and breathed in the cool air. It was nice to be able to see green grass for a change. She had the desire to go running through her secluded backyard celebrating with cartwheels and tumbles, knowing she wasn't going to be sinking into wet snow.

It was what she had done when she was young living with her dad. The talk about him saddened her and she wished he hadn't asked her about it.

Vince turned off the television and walked out to join her. He noticed the sadness in her eyes when he glanced at her and knew he'd brought up memories she didn't want to think about.

"Nice," he said, leaning over the white railing of the patio admiring her yard.

"Thanks." She grinned, standing beside him with the same stance. "It's home."

"It seems like it could get a little lonely here."

"Sometimes it can, but I'm rarely home anyway. I've been so busy since college I'm surprised I even remember my own address."

"You were touring with that rock band," he said pondering for a moment. "What was the name—Triton?"

She frowned slightly. "Yeah, Triton," she answered leaning her chin down on her hands.

"It must've been a bad situation." He turned his body towards hers.

"It wasn't terrible. I—" She glanced at him and suddenly smiled. "Never mind, it's silly."

"No, tell me." He nudged her elbow with his hand.

She stood up straight and leaned back on the railing. "Well, I was with the band for almost three years. It was a lot of fun, and a lot of hard work too." She smiled. "But Sam and I became close."

Vince nodded. "Ah, a little too close? And then he didn't want anything to do with you."

She waited for derogatory words, but they never came. Instead he looped his arm through hers and held her hand.

"So that's why you're so wishy-washy when it comes to relationships," he said as if realizing it for the first time. He sighed, kicking his foot lightly on the railing.

"Wishy-washy?"

"Yeah," he answered. "You want to give in to your emotions, but you won't let yourself because you're scared."

"I'm not scared." She shook her head and gave him a cynical laugh.

"Yes, you are. You're afraid you're going to get hurt so you keep yourself from forming any kind of personal relationship. That's a problem when you take on a client."

"Oh?" She looked intrigued by his assumption. "Do go on."

"In your line of work, personal and business relationships have to be intertwined to some degree. If we can't find a truce and be able to communicate with each other, we won't make it on a business level either."

"That doesn't mean it's alright to be with each other sexually."

He pulled her over to him and wrapped his arms around her shoulders with a smile. "You need to lighten up. Stop dwelling on what happened in the past or what will happen in the future." He gazed into her eyes. "Stop worrying about what's right or wrong, and listen to what your heart's telling you."

"If I do that—" She swallowed hard. "It might get broken."

"Then I'll be gentle with it," he whispered as he cupped her face in his hands and pulled her lips to his.

Completely taken by his words, she took his advice and decided to forget everything that had happened in the past and finally give in to him freely. *No guilt,* she told herself as he picked her up into his arms, kissing her vigorously as he carried her down the hallway.

"Which one's your room?" he asked, breathing fast, recklessly pulling at her lips.

"The last one," she breathed, "on the right."

No matter what happens, she thought as he frantically unbuttoned her shirt, she was not going to expect anything from him afterwards. She tried to think of more excuses to make, but when he carried her near the bed and dropped her to her feet in front of him, he stopped.

With her shirt completely unbuttoned, her bra unsnapped, and her chest heaving in excitement, she wondered what he was doing. Why had he stopped? She was beginning to feel a little awkward as he stared at her.

She folded her shirt over her exposed breasts and waited for something to happen. Anything at this moment would be nice.

Maybe he had changed his mind. Or worse yet, maybe he had been jokingly turning her into a sex-crazed nymph. She started to glare as the thought became more likely with each passing second.

He finally squeezed her shoulders gently and pulled her close to him, kissing her softly on the lips. It threw her completely off guard and she returned into the excited mess she was before. But this time he'd changed it into a slow, more romantic mood.

He was sensual, sliding his hands over her hips massaging them as he nuzzled her ear. She trembled as he moved his lips down her neck to her nipple and held his head as he grasped at it gently with his warm mouth.

His hair was soft in her hands, and it tickled when it touched her skin. She let her shirt and bra fall to the floor with her pants. Tension coursed through her entire body as she stood naked, willing and yearning for him to touch her.

The anticipation grew as she pulled his clothes off, one by one letting them fall to the floor. Mesmerized by his statuesque build, she couldn't take her eyes off of him.

He grinned at the expression on her face. "You like what you see?" he whispered as he picked her up into his arms. "I know I do."

She wrapped her legs around him as he took her to the bed and laid her down. His tongue dove into her mouth as he pressed his body against hers. He felt warm, delicious and undeniably hard.

Her mind was swept of everything, letting herself go completely. It was too late to turn back now anyway for she was completely engulfed in him.

As he ran his tongue down her body, he stopped to kiss around her navel. It sent her into a shy laugh.

He glanced up at her with a grin. "Ah, I found a ticklish spot." Growling playfully, he seemed to find pleasure in the small bumps that spread over her skin.

As he made his way back up to her mouth, she felt she would burst. The intense emotions she felt now were erotic, sensual, and finally relaxed with her thoughts.

"Just make love to me," she whispered in his ear, pulling on his skin with her lips.

She ran her hands down his back, feeling his muscles tense. He shifted his weight overtop of hers and then suddenly stopped.

"Are you sure you want to do this?" he asked softly, stroking her hair back away from her face and kissing her lightly on the temple.

It was an odd question for him to ask, but she respected it with a smile. Nobody had ever asked her that, especially when she had already passed the point of backing out.

Throwing her arms around his neck and wrapping her legs tighter around his waist, she sighed. "I want you."

There was no doubt about that. Regardless of the consequences, she wasn't going to let sex get in the way of business. Not this time. Convincing herself if he decided he'd never talk to her again after this, it would be fine with her. She could work around it this time.

A breath escaped her lips as he pushed inside her, making her lose her thoughts completely. He moved his hips slowly at first, indulging in the moment of their first time together.

She loved the way he enveloped her tongue with his, the way he touched her skin and stroked her hair. The way he moved was sensual, inviting and erotic in a sense that even the most provocative experience seemed dull to it.

He began to move faster, plunging and thrusting as if he were pushing her thoughts away. She found herself in a fit of euphoric gasps, aching for more of him as she held on tight.

Sweat beaded his body as he slid on her, holding her knee to his hip, massaging and squeezing every time he pushed. She wasn't going to last, especially since he found the perfect spot.

It was the one no one had ever touched before, the one she never knew she had until now. It was a sudden reaction when he hit it. She had never felt anything so wonderful. As the tingling sensation poured through her, taking her breath away, she moaned in ecstasy.

He brought her to a swift climax that sent her head spinning in delight. He caressed her body, cupping his hands gently on her breasts as he kissed her deeply, quieting her moans until she had to pull away and breathe.

Burying her face in his neck, she breathed hard, panting to catch the breath he so remarkably stole from her. The deep sensation in her stomach pulled at him, aching in fulfilled pleasure.

He breathed with her, calling out her name. She loved hearing it and smiled generously at him.

She lay underneath him, holding him. Running her fingers through his hair and down his strong arms, she felt the veins become erect with a quick pulse. She didn't want to let go as their breathing slowed down to a sweet melodic chant.

He kissed her as he lay back on the bed with a smile, keeping her in his embrace. He was beautiful, the most beautiful man she had ever been with. Although it had been a strange relationship from the start, it was stranger now that they were together.

What was going to come out of this now that she was completely taken by him? Was he going to leave her now that he got what he wanted?

She knew she had desperately wanted him, but she never dreamed she would ever feel this way, perfectly happy in his arms. A smile crept across her face as she laid her head on his chest. She wanted to squeeze him tightly and never move from that spot. They could stay there forever, making love all night, every night for all she cared.

Morgan gasped silently and shut her eyes tight. She had to get rid of those thoughts, because that was never going to happen. This was just a one-time thing. Sweet unbridled sex. And that was all.

"What's wrong?" Vince asked, breaking the silence in the room.

She opened her eyes. "Nothing," she lied, turning her face to his with an innocent smile.

He leaned down and kissed her. The way he stroked her hair made her body tingle all over again. And in no time, she found herself wanting more of him.

The day passed as he made love to her over and over. Each time they finished, they would start back up again by a touch or a simple kiss gone awry with passion.

She knew there was no way she'd make it in to the office, but she didn't care. Right now all she wanted was him, in her bed, making her feel like she was the most beautiful woman in the world.

And as he finished with a groaning laugh that it was their fourth time that day, she finally closed her eyes. She was completely exhausted.

He ran his fingers down her back, rubbing it softly. "It's dark outside." He grinned, propping his head up with his free hand. "Maybe we should stay here for the night."

They had been in bed for hours. His stamina was incredible, she thought happily as she yawned and closed her eyes slightly. "That's a good idea."

"Are you falling asleep?" he asked, tickling her lightly on her ribs.

"No, I'm not tired."

"Neither am I."

She thought for a moment, wanting to start a conversation. She yearned to hear him talk to her, to say romantic things—or anything for that matter, just as long as he kept her close to him.

"Why don't we discuss your personal agenda?" She eyed him curiously.

"Okay," he said with an intrigued voice. "I suppose you're going to ask me if we're an item now."

"No, I wasn't going to ask that."

She laughed nervously, although the thought had crossed her mind. And for some reason, the way he'd said it gave her the impression he wasn't looking for that kind of relationship. She knew when she let go of her emotions, not to expect anything more than sex.

"Forget about it," she continued. "It was just a silly attempt for conversation."

She turned over to her side, leaving his arms. Reaching for the bedspread that had fallen in the floor, she was stopped by his hand on her arm.

"Wait a second," he said and tugged at her to come back. "What did I say?"

"It's no big deal." Morgan cast a false grin, hoping it was good enough to fool him. "You didn't say anything wrong. I'm just getting the covers off the floor."

He sat up and pulled her over to him. "Come on, don't give me that. I know you're upset with me."

"How do you know?"

Chuckling, he ran his eyes over her face. He lifted his index finger to her cheek and pressed just above the corner of her lip.

"When you get mad," he said smiling. "You get this cute little dimple right here."

He leaned down and kissed her cheek lightly, sending her body trembling in delight. Stroking her hair, he pulled her body onto his as he leaned back, caressing her gently with his fingers and gazing into her eyes.

"When you're mad, your eyes turn a deep shade of blue, like the depths of the ocean. I get swept away in them," he said with a light voice.

His attempt to be romantically poetic was making her blush. She turned away from his stern eyes and laid her head down on his chest. Her heart raced, wanting him to say more, but he kept quiet.

"So what kind of things do you want to know about me?" he suddenly asked, his normal deep tone returning to his voice.

She thought for a moment and raised her head to look at him. "I don't know. I guess we can start with little things like, what is your favorite food?"

"It's what every good New York sportsman likes, a Coney Island chili dog and a beer. What about you?"

She grinned, thinking about the food at her favorite restaurant. "Vertoni's Chicken Alfredo."

"Never heard of it," he said, pulling at a strand of her hair that was tickling his chest.

"I don't get to go to Vertoni's often anymore, but the place has the best Italian food around. I'll take you there sometime."

"Somehow I figured you weren't a simple woman." He chuckled. "I'll bet your favorite color is Ocean Mist Blue. And I'm thinking you prefer bubble baths to showers, with candlelight and rose petals floating around you."

Morgan laughed. It sounded silly coming from him, but he was right in a way. A bubble bath sounded relaxing, but only if he joined her in the tub.

"You do, don't you?" He grinned, pushing her hair back from her face.

"No."

"Ah, I see that lying quiver in your eyes."

"Okay," she confessed. "Maybe the bath sounds interesting, but the color—" She twisted her lips. "I'm more of a violet kind of gal."

"Violet's cool," he said. "You'd look lovely with a lilac in your hair, walking down a white sandy beach in a white bikini." He took in a breath and propped his head up with his arm. "Damn, you'd look hot."

She laughed, shifting her weight to the side of him. "That's a typical male thought."

"Hey," he argued. "I'm entitled to have daydreams about you now."

"Oh, you are?"

"Sure. Men are supposed to daydream about women and vice versa." He turned over to his side. "I'd love to hear some of yours about me."

The sudden laugh that came out of her mouth shocked her. It was true she'd daydreamed about him, but she wasn't going to tell him that.

"Come on," he pleaded. "I told you one of mine, tell me one of yours."

"I don't have any."

"Yes, you do."

"No, I don't daydream."

"Oh, that's a blatant lie. Everyone daydreams."

Seeing that he was completely serious about hearing one, and wasn't going to give up, she sighed in defeat. A short laugh escaped her nose as she shook her head in amusement.

"Fine," she agreed. "I'll tell you one, but you have to promise not to laugh."

He positioned himself beside her as he propped his head up with his hand. With his eyes on her, completely enthralled with what she had to say, he grinned.

"Okay," she said, playing with the sheet as she nervously averted her eyes from his. "I envision the man of my dreams in a firefighter's uniform, gray with yellow stripes glowing in the sunlight and the helmet on his head. He has the upper part of the uniform pulled down, exposing his chest, but the suspenders are still over his shoulders. He's spraying the hose from the fire truck, but he's watering a garden full of roses. He looks over at me and smiles as he, in slow motion, turns the hose off and starts walking towards me. He grabs me up in his arms and swings me around through the garden."

She kept her eyes on the sheet she'd twisted tightly around her fingers afraid to see his reaction. The bed began to shake.

Finding the courage to do so, she looked up at him. He was trying desperately to keep from bursting into hysterics, making his body shake with his internal laughter until he finally couldn't hold it any longer.

"Oh man," he said laughing heartily. "That's pretty vivid."

"You jerk." She laughed with him. "You promised you wouldn't laugh." Her face turned red in embarrassment.

"I'm sorry." He gained composure, grabbing her hand before she could get out of bed. "No, don't leave."

"You're making fun of me."

"Oh, come on. I thought it was cute."

She let him pull her back over to him. He held her head in his hands, gazing down into her eyes with a smile.

"So, who is the dream guy?" he asked, kissing the lid of her eye.

"I don't know," she answered.

"Is it me?" he asked, breathing on her neck as he pulled at her skin softly with his lips.

"Maybe," she answered, closing her eyes.

He kissed her tenderly on her lips before he moved away from her and off of the bed. She watched him walk, the muscles in his hips and thighs tensing with his steps, sending her brows into an arch. Mesmerized by him, she hated to see his naked body disappear through the bathroom door.

"One more question," he yelled from the bathroom as he turned on the faucet.

"Okay," she yelled back at him.

"Tell me what happened on the mountain that night."

"Why do you have to bring that up?" she asked as he came to stand in the doorway staring at her with a towel wrapped around his waist.

"I just need to know," he answered. "I mean, I have my suspicions about it, but I need to hear it from you."

She folded her arms over her chest. "If you think you know, then why don't you tell me?"

"Okay, I think he wanted you to have sex with him. When you refused, he kicked you out of the car and left."

"You're quite the perceptive one aren't you? Since we're being so honest, why don't you tell me why you two are always in a pissing match?"

He walked over to the bed and sat down beside her. Running his hand up her leg until it rested on her knee, he smiled.

"We've been rivals for years. He just likes taking things a little too far."

"What kind of things?" she asked.

"I really don't want to talk about him anymore."

"You brought it up."

"I know. I know," he said dropping his hand from her knee. "I'm sorry I did."

He grinned as he stood up, pulling her with him. "Then let's not talk about it anymore."

She rose to meet his lips, smiling as he grabbed her behind and squeezed. He backed towards the bathroom, pulling her with him as they kissed.

"What's going on in here?" he asked, grinning mischievously. "Is that water I hear running into the tub?"

He picked her up in his arms and set her down in the large garden tub filled with bubbles. She pulled him down with her, splashing water into the floor.

"Sorry I didn't have any rose petals to spread around in the water."

He slid down beside her and turned the water off before it overflowed.

When he leaned back against the wall of the tub, she immediately moved her body overtop of him. Straddling his hips, she found him hard against her. With a quick move, she found her way on him, letting out a short gasp of pleasure.

"You didn't waste any time," he said, caressing her arms as she leaned back and forth on him.

"I couldn't resist your charm any longer." She put her wet, soapy arms around his neck.

"Honestly," he groaned closing his eyes. "I was wondering what was taking you so long."

"How many times is this?" she asked, moving a little faster, breathing a little harder as he began to move his hips upward, meeting her halfway.

"I've lost count." He pulled at her with his hands, massaging, caressing and squeezing her skin in the warm water.

Waves began to spill out onto the white tiled floor of the bathroom. Moans of pleasure, stolen breaths and an erotic dance broke out. Uniformed in bubbles, their bodies slipped together, creating an easier way to make love.

"Five," she breathed out hard in a whine, trying not to slip down the tub and away from his grasp.

He stared at her in humored awe, holding her hips down on him as he let out a growling, pleasured sigh. The thought of her calling a number out during their orgasmic ending turned his sigh into an eccentric laugh.

"Sorry," she apologized, laughing at his reaction as she tried to catch her breath. "I meant to say this is our fifth time today."

•

Stretching aimlessly across the bed, Morgan woke up with a smile. The sun was shining through her window followed by the sounds of chirping birds that hadn't left for the winter.

Vince wasn't there so she hopped out of bed to go find him. Hoping she'd find him on the back deck holding a cup of coffee out for her with a smile, she left the room sheathing herself in her robe.

Noticing there was no coffee in the small pot on the counter beside her refrigerator, she glanced around at the empty house.

He was gone.

She ran to the living room window and tossed open its sheer curtains. His truck wasn't in the driveway anymore. Her heart sank and she swallowed her tears.

"You knew this was going to happen." She scolded herself for even thinking of crying. She was not going to cry over the likes of him.

She scraped her feet across the carpet down the hallway and into her room. Crying was not an option. She pursed her lips into a scowl telling her to fight the tears back.

The jerk left her, and without a way back to the lodge, which was fine. She wasn't helpless. She could drive herself there and *then* break down into an uncontrollable bawl.

"No," she said aloud, gathering up clothes to wear for the day. She grabbed her undergarments from the top drawer, black slacks and matching blouse from the bedroom closet, a towel from the linen closet—and her heart from the floor as she went to the bathroom for a shower.

The heat from the water steamed up the mirror hanging from the shower head. At least she couldn't see the tears creeping into her eyes.

The scent of him still lingered on her skin as if he was still with her. She felt she could melt and wash down the drain as she squeezed out a few tears from her eyes. Warm as the water over her head, more and more tears came out until she was finally bursting in heartache.

Why did she have to go through this again? Deep down, she thought for sure he was going to be different, but it seemed he was completely typical. He had only been out for one thing, and she fell for it.

She wanted to be angry, but her heart wouldn't let her. She cried furiously and would've stayed there forever if the water hadn't started to turn cold.

Opening the bathroom door, a smell wafted into her nose.

"Bacon?"

She wrapped the towel around her body and slowly inched down the hall to the kitchen to investigate. She found her way into the dining room and plunked herself down at the table in awe.

The small round table she rarely used was set in perfect proportions. With a plate of fresh strawberries, a stack of steaming pancakes, a stem of ripened bananas and a jug of orange juice, the table screamed breakfast.

She wondered how he had time to do it. It was set so beautifully, not to mention organized perfectly around a clear glass vase coupled with the most beautiful long-stemmed red roses she had ever seen.

He was cooking bacon on the stove, grinning ear to ear, glancing back at her as he moved them around in the sizzling pan. "I hope you're hungry." He turned over one of the greasy limp slices.

Morgan sat quietly, not knowing exactly what to say. He had shocked her so much all she could do was sit there still dripping and hanging on to the towel around her body.

He hurried to the table and poured her a glass of orange juice. "Have you been crying?" He leaned down and looked at her worriedly.

"No." She shrugged, trying to escape her mesmerized stare at all the food.

"Yes, you have." He pulled her up off the chair and took her into his arms.

"I thought you left me," she blurted out. She tried not to, but tears welled in her eyes again.

"Damn." He shook his head with guilt. "I wanted to wake you, but you were sleeping so soundly. I thought I'd be back before you woke, but the traffic—well, you know how traffic is here."

He leaned down and kissed her lightly on the lips. "I'm not that bad of a guy." He grinned.

Morgan cracked a smile. She wanted to stay in his arms, let him take her back to the bedroom and make love to her the rest of the day, but his bacon was burning.

"You like your bacon crispy?" she asked, glancing at the smoke billowing from the pan.

Curses and mumbles escaped his mouth, followed by disappointing talks of everything going to the garbage as he quickly turned off the burner. "Without bacon, a breakfast is bland," he said as if nothing was edible at all.

Morgan had already sat down and started into the sweet juicy strawberries, and was about to topple her plate with pancakes when Vince stopped her. He brought her to her feet and pulled her clutched hand off her towel, making it drop to the floor.

"Oops," he said with a sheepish grin. He enjoyed it as her white silky skin flushed red when she stood there in front of him completely naked. "You're so beautiful," he whispered, sliding his fingers down her arms and clasping his hands into hers. "I'm sorry I left without telling you."

He pulled her gently towards him, pressing his warm body against hers. The feeling rushed through her again as he slid his hands down her stomach, passing over her thighs and then down her legs. He retrieved her towel off the floor and then stood back up.

The sense of giddiness, and above all wanting him right then and there, returned to her like the water from a newly broken dam and washed away every bad emotion from her. As he wrapped the towel back around her, smiling down into her eyes, the sensation grew.

"Maybe you should get dressed so we can eat," he whispered just before he kissed her again on the lips.

She agreed with a nod and turned around to leave. She walked down the hallway to her room with her head swimming. The weakness in her knees caught up with her as she sat down on the edge of the bed and cried.

She hadn't meant to let her tears loose again, but she couldn't help it. There was no way she could go back to business as usual now. And although she was completely taken with him, she wasn't so sure that was a good thing.

Chapter 10

Evans Ridge Lodge was built in 1952 on one of the most advantageous mountains in New York. It was originally called Schaffer's Lodge, named after the first owners—one of the richest families in New England.

On its opening, the lodge became an instant success and catered to skiers of all types, but mostly to the celebrities and baby boomers of the fifties. At one time, even President Kennedy had taken up residence in one of the suites, which was later named President's House.

It had become so popular eventually the Schaffer's turned the entire lodge into a gated community and nobody could stay there unless they had reservations or were well established in the public eye. In other words, they had to be rich and famous.

That had all changed in one tragic day in 1960. After one of the biggest storms hit the coast of Maine, it brought in a blizzard that dumped well over forty feet at the lodge and even more on the mountain above.

People were stranded, although it wasn't quite unusual for that to happen. But after the second day, an avalanche barreled through the lodge, killing many people.

Some said God had cleansed the mountain that day, wiping away greed and corruption with one swift wave of His hand. Others believed it saved the mountain, because afterwards the Schaffers reopened it to everyone. Of course, it was also noted that most of the celebrities didn't want anything to do with the place anymore and big business for the Schaffers was dwindling.

In turn, the Schaffers sold it to Ed and Emma and they renamed it Evans Lodge. After a few additions, including a medical wing and a helicopter pad on the roof, it was reopened to the public and became the quiet, friendly place it was now.

Morgan loved that story, as horrible as it was. She loved to tell it as an icebreaker to sponsors who were willing to listen. And as she stood on the roof and watched the helicopter land, she was prepared to make it a conversation piece again.

It was an amazing sight to see. The rotation of the propellers whipped snow into her face, stinging it with a forceful blow. She was happy her guests had made it safely.

The heat from the lodge was inviting. She pulled her gloves and earmuffs off and welcomed them with a smile.

"We only have a few hours to take the live action shots, so we're going to have to hurry," one of the men said standing along side his camera equipment. "I really apologize for the inconvenience of being a week late."

"No need to worry. Vince is ready for you."

She led the small group, which took pictures as they walked through the lodge to a Crawler that was waiting to take them up the mountain to the halfpipe. She told them the history behind the place on the way up, and was glad to see they were just as intrigued by it as she was.

After the crew loaded their equipment they made the trek to a small clearing where Vince was already doing stunts. With instant grins at his agility on a snowboard, they set up the cameras and began snapping pictures.

"I was pleased to hear he's a last-second qualifier for the Winter Games," the representative overseeing the shoot told Morgan. "I was shocked actually. I don't think there's ever been anyone accepted this close to time."

"I know," Morgan replied with a smile. "He's worked hard for it. If anyone deserves it, it's him."

"He must have a good manager," he said. He performed perfectly in front of them. Morgan loved it. She heard one of them comment on how difficult his signature jump looked, and she agreed.

As he finished with a ten-eighty, it sent the cameras into a fit of flashing. He left everyone on the mountain breathless, including Morgan.

After Vince met with the representative for a short interview in the closed off restaurant of the lodge, he sighed in relief. Listening to the helicopter leave, he glanced at the clock. It was already ten PM, although it felt later than that, and he was completely worn out.

"I don't know how people manage this on a daily basis," he said.

Morgan smiled, walking behind him up the winding lobby stairs. "You'll get used to it."

"Honestly, I could do without the famous factor of my career. The entire day feels wasted."

"Not wasted," Morgan replied as she bit into the apple she'd been carrying since they left the restaurant. "It's for the sake of gold, my dear."

"Yeah, whatever," he said. He stretched his sore arm over his chest as he walked. It had been the longest he'd stayed on the half-pipe, and he was beginning to feel it in his muscles.

"Oh, that reminds me," she spoke with her mouth full of apple bits as they neared his room. "The production company will be here in two weeks to shoot the commercial."

He blinked at her, half understanding her and half not wanting to hear. "A commercial?" He unlocked his door and they stepped inside the room.

"Yeah." She looked puzzled. "Didn't I tell you about it this morning?"

"No."

"I know I told you about it." She grabbed her laptop from the bar and sat down on the couch beside him cursing through her teeth. "The Winter Sky Lip Balm Company will be here on December fifteenth to shoot their new commercial."

She glanced up at him, hoping he wasn't going to be mad at her for what she had to tell him. Realizing she had indeed forgotten, she choked slightly on her apple.

"Are they going to film in the lodge?" he asked.

"Not exactly." She held her hand to her temple in quiet contemplation. The only way to tell him was just to blurt it out and take the consequences of her neglect in stride. "They're going to film on the halfpipe—" Her voice trailed as she saw his wide-eyed reaction.

"Say again?" He rubbed his shadowed jaw.

"I meant to tell you, but I've been so busy today I completely forgot."

He paced the room in front of the roaring fire, and stopped to stoke it with a wrought iron poker. He didn't look aggravated, but she could tell by his sudden urge to pace again he was getting there.

"When will they be here?"

"November fifteenth. That's in two weeks." She cringed. "You're mad now aren't you?"

He stopped pacing and grinned at her. "I don't mind them shooting a commercial here." He sat down beside her and put his arms around her. "As long as it doesn't cut into practice, they can do whatever they want."

She grinned guiltily. He was going to love what she had to tell him next. Feeling his arms around her, she thought maybe it could wait. But since they were already on the subject, she had to just get it over with.

"By the way—" She glanced up at the ceiling as if she was talking to herself about it, and preferably so for this matter. "You might have a small part in the commercial."

He twisted his lips to the side. "I might?"

"Well, you do actually."

She smiled innocently as he released her from his arms and stood back up. She watched him move to the fire and turn his backside to it.

"I have to actually *be* in this commercial?"

"I'm really sorry. It's not like me to forget things like this."

"How small of a part?" he asked in a stern, monotone voice.

"Just two or three lines." She swallowed hard.

She gathered her unfinished apple, laptop, and her pride and started for the door.

"What do I have to say?" he asked, clearing his throat.

"I'll print out your lines and give them to you tomorrow," she said as she passed in front of him. But before she could leave, he grabbed her by the arm and pulled her to him.

"Where are you going?"

Glancing up into his eyes, she smiled. "I thought maybe you might want to be alone—to get over being mad about the commercial."

He chuckled at the nervous twitch in her cheek. "I trust you. If I'm to be in a commercial you set up, then I'll do it."

He reached around her and pulled the clip out of her rolled up hair. He watched as the long strands fell down around her shoulders. He lifted her up off her feet and carried her to the couch and laid her down, toppling her. He stroked her hair as he nuzzled her ear.

She closed her eyes, enjoying the warmth of his breath though she knew she shouldn't. She relinquished her things from her hands, letting them slide to the floor, and wrapped her arms around him.

"I shouldn't be this close to you," she said, sighing as he breathed on her ear. She held on to him tightly wanting him in a terrible way.

"Even after our breakthrough at your house, you still fight your feelings," he replied without hesitating.

"I can't give in to you again," she said pushing him up off of her.

"You're killing me, Morgan," he said and sat up. "One minute you want to be with me, then the next you're running away."

She scowled. "I'm just trying to be rational and quit before it ends in a big disaster."

"Before what ends?" he asked.

"This relationship."

He quickly grabbed her hand before she could get up and leave. He pulled her back down on the couch and looked as though he'd just won the argument.

"This relationship will not end," he said, squeezing her arms gently as he eyed her seductively.

"It will." She swallowed hard as he stared at her with seriousness in his eyes.

"No, it won't," he said as he pulled her closer, inching his lips towards hers.

"It will," she replied as she let him move her towards him.

"It won't," he whispered.

"It might." She got her last word in just before he touched his lips to hers.

She didn't hold back as he enveloped her in his arms and pulled her across his lap. As she embraced him, he massaged her side, her hip, and pulled her tucked-in shirt from her slacks. The increasing desire she had for him intensified when he pulled her underneath him and began unbuttoning her blouse as he continued with his luscious kiss.

But as she lost herself in her emotions, the moment came to an abrupt end when someone knocked on the door loudly. She looked at him in disappointment, but also in relief that it brought her back to her senses.

He hesitated to get up to answer it and continued pulling at her lips with his and fondling her gently under her shirt. He knew exactly what made her weak as he found her nipple with his thumb.

But when a much harder knock came to the door, he stopped. With a heaving sigh, he pulled himself up from the couch. A growl escaped his lips as she buttoned her shirt back up.

With one last glance at her to make sure she'd gathered her composure, his face fell flat. He hated to see her tuck her shirt back in and tie her hair back up into its usual folded 'do.

Vince swung the door open to their bothersome guest. "Chad."

"Hey bro," he said as he walked in, grinning with a proud smirk. "What's going on?"

Vince eyed Morgan. "Not much."

Morgan could see the annoyed look in his eyes, and she imagined she carried the same expression as Chad sat on the couch next to her. If only he'd come an hour later. But maybe he'd been her savior, keeping her from making that big mistake.

"Hey beautiful," Chad said grinning at Morgan's heaving chest.

Realizing his eyes had wandered to the two erect lumps poking from her white blouse, she quickly stood up and walked to the door. "I'll see you later, Vince. I have some work to catch up on."

"I'll stop by your room tomorrow. " He kissed her lightly on the lips before she left with her stomach in knots.

She hurried to her room and shut the door behind her. She set down her laptop on the table and then fell onto the bed with a groan.

Frustrated and completely starving for his touch, she turned over on her back and stared at the ceiling. She had to think of something else.

She grabbed her laptop from the table and turned it on. She hooked up her printer, printed out his lines for the commercial and slipped the paper into an envelope for safekeeping.

Bored again, she leaned back on the bed and closed her eyes. Smiling at the thought of him again, she turned out the light beside the bed and quickly fell asleep.

•

Morgan awoke to the in-house phone ringing in her ear. Groaning, she wished she'd moved it to the other side of the room. Happy it had stopped after the fourth ring, she tried to go back to sleep.

It rang again. This time Morgan sat up at the edge of the bed and angrily answered. "What?"

"I'm sorry to bother you so early." The morning shift clerk squeaked out an apology. Morgan could hear commotion in the background and wondered what was going on.

Had she slept through two weeks and the television crew was here to film the commercial? Morgan glanced at the large numbered digital clock beside the phone. It was seven-thirty.

"No bother. What can I do for you?" Morgan yawned.

"There's someone here insisting on seeing you." The woman giggled as the voices grew louder in the background.

"I'll be down in a few minutes."

She hung up the phone. Maybe Sally or Regina had come to visit her. As she stepped down the stairs, she suddenly couldn't wait to see Sally. God knew she needed some female conversation.

As she neared the lobby, there was so much chatter she thought a women's convention was going on. Puzzled, she stopped at the hallway and searched the small crowd gathered around someone.

"Who is that?" Morgan moved through the excited crowd of people until she caught glimpse of long black hair. Her eyes widened in shock at the sight of his smiling face as he signed autographs for the crowd around him.

It was him. He was here, looking for her. She pinched herself to see if she was dreaming, but the stinging sensation didn't wake her up. No, she was still there covering her face with her hands in complete astonishment that he, Sam Triton, was actually here.

She tried not to tremble as he caught glimpse of her and grinned ear to ear. She lowered her hands from her shocked face as he made his way over to her.

"Sam?" she said as he came at her with open arms.

"Morgan." He hugged her tightly with a happy sigh.

"What are you doing here?" She pushed him away to look at him. "How—"

Sam shushed her by pressing his finger to her lips. "Let's talk in private."

Morgan hadn't noticed the crowd of people gathered around both of them. With a grin, she led him up the stairs to her room.

As soon as the door closed, he twirled her around and planted a kiss on her lips. She wasn't sure what to do, but it had happened so fast she couldn't stop it.

He broke away, cupping her face in his palm, and gazed into her eyes. "I've missed you so much," he whispered, lightly pecking on her cheek.

"I can't say I've missed you, Sam." She walked to the bed and began to make it up.

"I deserve that." He took off his jacket and crashed into the recliner with a grunt. "I really wasn't sure what to do with you back then. You wanted something I couldn't give you."

She gave out a surprised laugh.

"Whether you believe it or not, I cared about your feelings." He chuckled, amused at her attempt to cover up her trembling hands.

She thought for a moment while folding a T-shirt. "If you really cared that much, how come you didn't talk to me afterwards?"

Sam sighed and leaned his head back on the recliner. She watched him with a keen eye still trying not to believe he was in her room.

"What are you doing here, Sam?"

"I came up here because I have a proposition for you," he said in a tone she'd never heard him use before. It was professional, business like, and quite striking from him.

"I'm listening." She sat down on the corner of the bed. As intriguing as it might be, she knew she couldn't accept—she wouldn't.

Sam sat up and looked her straight in the eyes. "The new album's coming out early next year, and I need you to set up things overseas. The consultant I hired has no idea how to do her job." He shook his head and leaned back in the chair. "I want you coordinating with me. We'd be doing this together."

"Together?" She was stunned. Although flattered, she knew there was no way she could carry two clients at once. "I can't Sam. I'm under a contract here. Plus, I like it very much."

Sam glanced at the newly folded clothes. "You're still a slob I see. I don't think I've ever seen you fold your clothes before."

"Listen, I realize you made a long trek up here, but I can't get out of my contract right now. I don't want out of it."

"Why don't you look at me?"

"I am looking at you," she said, fixing her eyes on his.

With his long black hair over his flawlessly muscular body, she remembered what it was that had attracted her to him. But the feelings she'd carried for him before were nowhere to be found.

"I can't and won't take you up on your offer." She grinned, finding it easy to turn him down. "Somehow, I know I belong here. I'm comfortable and quite happy."

"Wow," he said, the look of shock spreading across his face. "What's wrong with you? You're not the Morgan I remember."

"What's that supposed to mean?"

"I've never known you to want to be comfortable at home. You're a risk-taker, a woman with a plan that'll knock people over when you walk through a room. Thinking on your feet is what you do best, and that's why I'm willing to pay you whatever you want."

"I appreciate the compliment, but I really am quite satisfied here."

"Did you hear what I said?" he asked, ignoring her answer again. "I'll pay you anything you want. A hundred thousand, a million. I don't care. I need you."

"You'd pay me a million?" She laughed.

"If that's your price," he said leaning back in the recliner. "I'm good for it."

She shook her head. "If you agree to that, I'd say you need an accountant to manage your money better."

"I'm quite wealthy now." He looked her square in the eyes. "All I need is three months of your time, and then you can come back to this little hole you've climbed in."

She scowled. "I don't appreciate that comment, and my answer is—"

"Don't," he interrupted. "Don't give me your answer right now. I've decided to stay here for a few days and hopefully talk you into it. Maybe I can talk to this client of yours and convince him to let you go, just for the time I need you. I'll offer him money."

"You can't buy my contract from him. He won't agree to it."

"Everyone has a price," he said as he stood up from the chair and walked toward the door. "I'm staying in the President's Room, which is rather small considering the places I've stayed in. I'll come over after I grab a nap. Maybe we can do dinner."

She watched him leave. She knew Vince wouldn't let her go. He had a qualifying run coming up for the Olympics as well, so there'd be no way she could leave for three months. If she even gave the slightest indication she wanted to take Sam up on his offer, it would end up as a permanent leave. And she didn't want to go anywhere else but back into Vince's arms.

•

"I hate the cold weather." Sam shivered as he followed Morgan inside the building.

"You get used to it," she called back as she led him in to the restaurant.

The lunch traffic had taken most of the tables, but she spotted an empty one in the very back of the room and hurriedly guided him towards it. Word had spread throughout the lodge that he was there, and the place suddenly became littered with people.

Dressed in a tan winter coat and a black toboggan over large dark sunglasses, he was perfectly disguised. The only thing that could give him away was the fact his large muscular frame stood out from the typical crowd.

As they sat down, she was glad everyone went on about their lunch. Chattering and clanging of dishes from the kitchen covered up his deep booming voice as he began to talk to her again about his business deal.

"I told you I'm not interested," she snapped. "Vince is going to the Olympics in February. Since I'm his manager, not yours, he needs me here."

"Come on Morgan," he begged, pulling his sunglasses off his face. "If he's already accomplished what you came here for, there's no sense in sticking around."

She watched as he set the glasses near the edge of the table.

Running her eyes upward, she focused on the man walking towards them. It was Vince.

She'd sent a message to him to meet her for lunch in hopes to get their meeting out of the way. She only hoped he wouldn't get the wrong idea of what Sam was doing there.

A lump formed in her throat as she held her breath. He had his eyes, stern and perplexed, on her and the man sitting across from her. With a short frown, he stopped at their table.

"Vince," she said, scooting over to make room for him to sit down. "I want you to meet someone."

Vince sat down and took off his gloves. He reached over the table and offered his hand. "Sam Triton."

Sam smiled wide and shook his hand generously. "Yeah, and you must be Vince?"

Vince nodded as he released his hand. "It's nice to meet you."

Morgan was about to keel over. The tension inside her made her ill with nervousness. She only hoped that Sam would keep his mouth shut about the offer he gave her, but she knew that was too much to ask from the outspoken man.

"So." Vince eyed Morgan curiously. "What's going on?"

"I'd like to offer you a deal." Sam suddenly beamed, interrupting Morgan's protest. "But," he added. "I'd like to talk to you about it in private."

Vince tossed him a puzzled glance, noticing he was staring at Morgan. He followed his gaze and caught her look of disdain.

"No," she blurted out.

"Oh, come on Morgan," Sam insisted. "We won't be long."

"Vince," she said, wanting to take hold of his hand to keep him there, but he'd already stood up from the table.

Sam gave her a quick wink before he followed Vince out into the lobby and disappeared behind the wall. Her heart sank. She only hoped Vince would listen with a deterrent ear to what he had to say.

This wasn't right. She got up from the table and hurried out of the restaurant. When she saw them by the lobby doors she stopped, leaned on the banister of the stairs, and watched them talk among themselves.

Sam was definitely talking the talk, wheeling and dealing as if he were some slick car salesman. The half-grin he wore seemed to tell her somehow, he was getting somewhere.

She turned her eyes to Vince who stood with his arms folded over his chest, glancing down at the floor, obviously in thought as he listened. She wished she could hear what was being said, especially since he nodded in agreement over something.

Vince gave a short grin, shook Sam's hand and began walking towards her. His smile turned to frown as he glared at her intently, straightening his gloves in his hand as he neared the stairs.

She opened her mouth to ask what they'd talked about, but he moved his eyes forward and walked right by her. This time, her heart sank to the floor. Whatever he'd heard, he believed. And though she never knew Sam to lie about anything, there was obviously something not right about the situation.

"What the hell?" Morgan asked Sam as he came to stand in front of her with an ear to ear grin. "What'd you say to him?"

He chuckled. "I told him I'd take you off his hands for a few months. He's agreed to let you out of your contract completely. I told him you needed more money then what he's paying you."

"Sam." She tried to keep her voice calm and the tears from forming in her eyes. "I told you I didn't want to take your offer. You know I don't need money."

She turned to the stairs and began walking up, heading to Vince's room so she could explain. Anger loomed in her eyes as she glanced back at Sam.

"If you really didn't want to take the offer, you would've stopped me from talking to him," Sam said, grabbing her hand and stopping her from going further up the steps. "Honestly, you're not happy here. You deserve to be traveling and making your fortune. He doesn't deserve you."

With the glare she gave him, he dropped her hand from his grasp.

"I'm sorry," he spoke with concern. "I'm only trying to do what's best for you."

She suddenly looked away from his uneasy stare. Not wanting to believe him, she took another step up.

"I know you had feelings for him, so I'm truly sorry for you."

"I'll explain you've lost your mind completely," she said as she moved up the steps feeling his eyes on her back. "He'll understand."

"Go talk to him then," Sam called after her. "I'll be in my room when you're ready to leave."

She sauntered down the hallway and stopped at the door to his room. Raising her hand to a fist, she hesitated to knock, trying to find the words to say to him. Knowing it wouldn't be hard to tell him she was staying, she grinned and knocked on the door.

She'd only waited a moment and the door opened to Vince's somber gaze. He looked incredibly hurt and completely irritated.

"Hey," she said, watching him walk back into the room. "Are you okay?"

He sat down at the wooden bar. A bottle of tequila and a shot glass was set before him.

"Talk to me, Vince," she said. She moved in front of his stare and gathered his eyes on her.

"Well," he said, "shouldn't you be packing?"

She shook her head and smiled. "I'm not going anywhere."

"Yes, you are," he argued coldly. "I already tore up your contract."

Tears formed in her eyes. "Why'd you do that?"

"What do you think I am? Stupid?" He raised his growling voice. "He'll pay you better than I ever could. Since that's all that concerns you, you're free to leave."

"I don't want his money," she yelled. "I don't care about money, but I do care about you."

"That may be, but it's a little too late for that, don't you think?"

"I don't understand. It's a little too late for what?"

"Just leave. I'm done with you."

"Why are you so angry with me?" she asked, wiping tears from her cheeks. "I want to stay with you."

He raised his cold stare to her tear-filled eyes. He shrugged his shoulders. "I don't want you here anymore."

"Whatever Sam said to you, you can't listen to it," she pleaded. "He thinks he knows what's best for me, but he doesn't."

She tried to touch his arm but he moved it away. A sigh escaped her agape mouth.

"I thought we had something," she whispered. "The night we shared at my house, are you saying that meant nothing to you? It meant something to me."

He kept his eyes on the shot glass in front of him. Without a word, he downed it quickly, ignoring her. The silent treatment—it definitely wasn't the time for it.

"Fine," she blurted, trying to control her trembling voice. "If you're too ignorant to figure it out, then I'm leaving."

"Good." He threw her a blank stare. "That's what I've wanted all along."

"You're a liar," she snapped.

She ran from the room and slammed the door, not knowing what to do. Sliding down his door, she sat down on the floor and cried in her hands. She couldn't believe this. It just didn't seem right he was dumping her like this. It didn't make any sense at all.

It was Sam's horrible timing. If he hadn't shown up, none of this would be happening.

Maybe it was true Vince had used her. He'd hired her to do a job, and making her think he cared was just an added bonus to keep her on the move for his career. That was all she was to him, a glorified door mat that had helped him make it into the Winter Games. She wasn't needed anymore.

She rose to her feet. With tears still streaming her cheeks, she walked to her room, unlocked the door and went inside. Falling down into the recliner, she closed her eyes.

She knew what she had to do. It seemed the only option. She had to pack her bags, find Sam and go with him overseas. And the farther away she got from Vince, the better it'd be to get over him.

Chapter 11

Diamond heart earrings sparkled in the luminescent light of the large chandelier above the dinner table. Casting radiant colors on Morgan's black dress, her eyes were dazzled at the sight of them.

"It's for Christmas," he said smiling.

"But it's Thanksgiving, Sam."

"I know. I couldn't help it."

"Thank you," she said. As no other woman she knew could or would do, she closed the box and gave it back to him. "For safe keeping." She smiled, seeing Sam's bewildered look at her reaction to his expensive gift.

"Why don't you put them on?"

"Not here in front of the guests."

It was bad enough to have a formal Thanksgiving party together, but after numerous attempts to get it through Sam's thick skull they were strictly platonic, he still acted as though they were married. At least some times were like that. The other times were spent dragging him out of bed from all the women he slept with.

She wasn't at all unappreciative of his gift. His heart was always in the right place, but, as she thought, it was mostly in his pants.

The guests around the large table were supposed to be formal, yet they were as grungy as usual. Sam's band was meticulous for staying greasy even in their handsome black and white tuxedos.

Even the women on their arms looked like they hadn't slept in a month by the mascara smeared under their eyes. In tight above the knee, cleavage billowing out strapless dresses, they toppled over their greasy rich crushes, like dolls gone awry.

Morgan loved Sam's house. Secluded in the hills and just off a small lake in Illinois, it was a place she thought she could see herself retiring in.

The house was a white Victorian with round castle-like peaks built with dark gray brick. Large white pillars held the overhanging roof of the wrap-around porch, which made it the perfect rendition of a nineteenth century house.

When Sam bought it after his first album went gold, he had taken her with him to look at the house, insisting if she loved it, so did he. She had seen the glitter in his eyes when he realized there were horse stables behind the house. If there was one thing that nobody else knew about him but her, it was his love for horses.

Dinner was finally being served, and Morgan couldn't wait. She watched as the caterers set the dining table, which was fit for a king and his men with a large brown and succulent looking turkey.

She watched them eat like pigs. They used their fingers to pull on piled high turkey. They tossed rolls to each other, and passed bowls back and forth until every last bit was gone.

Morgan saw one of the caterers dressed in a white suit and hat roll his eyes slightly as he glanced at the ripped up shell of the turkey at the end of dinner. Obviously he had never served people as uncontrolled and half drunk as them.

Staring out the window after dinner, she wondered what Vince's Thanksgiving was like. The snow falling outside the window reminded her of the time at the lodge. She missed it with an ache in her heart. It had only been a few weeks, but it felt like it had been a year.

"Stop thinking about him," she told herself as she turned on the television.

Often she would turn it to the sports network during their winter coverage of events. That's how she learned of Vince's first place in the annual festival event on Mount Hood, Oregon just the weekend before. She wished she could've been there to see him perform.

She walked up the cherry stained stairs, running her fingers over the smooth wood. Maybe she should've gone to the bar with the rest of them.

She eyed her cell phone, trying not to think of Vince again. Maybe one call to his mother would be okay. Although she hadn't talked to any of them since she left that day with Sam, she knew Emma would be happy to hear from her. At least she hoped anyway.

Maybe she really wouldn't want to talk to her after everything that had happened. She wondered if she even knew Vince had kicked her to the curb.

She turned to her side facing away from her phone as if that would keep her from picking it up. It would be rude of her though if she didn't call and at least wish them a happy Thanksgiving.

At that thought, she grabbed her phone and dialed Emma's number. The pounding in her chest grew when she heard her voice.

"Emma, this is Morgan," she blurted out in hopes the next thing she wouldn't hear was a click from the sweet lady hanging up on her.

"Morgan, dear." Emma's voice grew with excitement. "It's so wonderful to hear from you. How are you doing?"

She breathed a sigh of relief. "I'm fine, just fine."

"How was your Turkey day? Did you eat too much?"

"It was fine." She hated lying and hoped Emma wouldn't hear it in her wavering voice. "How was yours?"

She belted out a raspy laugh. "Oh you know, the boys are here with Ed and me and we're just lounging around completely stuffed now." She gave a brief pause and then whispered. "Do you want to speak to Vince? He just hasn't been the same since you left. He's so cold shouldered."

"No." Morgan closed her eyes feeling weak in the knees to know that he was even there. "I just wanted to say hello."

"You know, he hired himself a new manager a few days ago.

She's here too, but I don't like her. I don't like her at all. She dresses like a floozy and hangs all over Vince like he's a bar in a closet."

A new woman in his life after just a few weeks, Morgan thought jealously. "Is he doing okay? How was his qualifier run?"

"Oh, he did wonderful. The American team accepted him after he broke a few records. I'm so proud. And I'm proud of you for straightening him out, too." She hesitated with a sigh. "He's terribly depressed though. I just hope he doesn't let his poor attitude take over again and get himself in trouble."

The jealous tendencies faded back into depression as she thought of him at the Olympics without her. Instead, he'd be competing with someone who didn't deserve to be with him.

"Well, I'll talk to you soon Emma. Please, give my regards to Ed for me, too."

"I will." Emma's voice smiled. "You take care now."

Morgan ended the call. She should've known better than to talk to her, but the urge was too overwhelming.

Vince. She had to get him out of her mind otherwise she was going to explode and crumble. Her heart already felt like it had been dug out with the dull blade of a plastic knife, but she didn't need anymore problems in her life.

Sam was just in a league of his own and not her type to say the least. He had tried so desperately lately for her to open up to him. Asking her over and over why she always looked unhappy.

Morgan sprawled out on the bed and stared at the tiled ceiling giving her self an ultimatum. Either she forget about Vince completely, or she'd never be alive inside again.

"But how can I truly be alive without him?"

Groaning and unable to close her eyes to go to sleep, she jumped out of bed, grabbed her laptop and fled down the two flights of stairs. She found the small breakfast table in the rounded nook at the back of the kitchen and opened her laptop.

She clicked a file from the screen and it opened with the dates Sam's other manager had e-mailed her. She knew she had to get to work on setting up their flight to England. It was the kick-off spot for their *Fish in Shallow Water Tour.*

Morgan laughed out loud, trying not to spit out the gulp of wine she'd just doused her mouth with. Their tour name was silly to her and she wondered exactly which one had come up with it. But she had to hand it to them that it was rather catchy and strangely went along with the band's name.

December sixth was their first concert and everything had to be set up by then. Kicking off in a famous London pub was exciting and unnerving at the same time.

"It'll be a learning experience for all of us," Sam said, offering up encouragement. But Morgan still thought they looked like scared little boys trying to get up the nerve to ask a girl to dance.

Passports had been their first priority. Although one of them had tried to have their picture taken cross-eyed, it had gone smoothly just a few days before the holiday.

Morgan sighed at the dates. Every Friday night from December to the end of January was filled. That didn't include setting up in coliseums, traveling and of course, sightseeing. That was something she couldn't wait for.

She was thought of as their good luck charm. Before going out on stage, the entire band would rub her head. It messed up her hair and she never liked the fact she had become something sacred to them. She was their angel, Sam always said.

Morgan smiled. It would be nice to get out of the country for awhile. She had wanted to see Stonehenge and the Eiffel Tower, but she'd definitely pass it up just to see Stockholm, Sweden. It wasn't so much about the place, it was more about the chocolate festival at the same time they were.

A sudden craving for it crept through her blurring eyes. She hadn't realized she'd drunk the entire bottle of wine until she stood up from the table and stumbled, laughing at herself as she made her way back to her room.

It was a tough climb, but once she was there, she crashed down on her bed, sobbing again at the thought of being so far away from everything and everyone she cared about. And the face that popped up in her head the most was Vince's.

Chapter 12

The British tour was completely overwhelming. They'd spent three weeks touring England, catching in large crowds in small, unbelievably packed smoky bars where the atmosphere was tremendously arousing.

Morgan couldn't help but enjoy every minute of the music blaring amongst screaming fans. It had been wonderful to hear Sam's echoing, booming, haunting voice again. It had made her skin rise in excited delight during each song he sang. And his grin was a sweet sensation that impaled the angry, heavily dark music the band played.

Although the tour had only just started, she was ready to go back to the states. And she was ever so happy the opportunity had finally come with Sally's wedding. She'd wanted to go alone, but Sam insisted on joining her.

As she stared out the window on the way to the airport, she thought of home. It had felt like an eternity since she'd been there and wished that she could stay. She was going to bring it up to Sam, since he really didn't need her touring with him any longer anyway.

She missed her house, her plants, but most of all she missed the lodge. Staying on the snowy mountain, sitting in front of a fire every night cuddling up with the man she loved under a thick wool blanket sounded heavenly, especially since it was so close to Christmas. But she knew that's all it was, just a wish that would never come true.

"Would you stop?" Sam insisted, pulling her over to sit beside him.

"What?" She rested her chin on his arm with a grin.

He clasped his hand in hers. "You look miserable again."

"I'm just tired I guess."

He squeezed her hand. "You wish you were getting married too, don't you?"

She puckered her lips with a noisy huff. "That's the most absurd thing you've ever said, Sam."

"Is it?"

"Maybe not the most absurd, but you should know by now I'm not ever going to get married."

"I don't believe that." He turned his body towards her and stared into her eyes. "You could marry me?"

She was thrown completely off guard. All she could do was stare at him in complete and utter awe. Speechless for the first time in her life that Sam of all people had popped the question.

"You don't have to answer now. Just think about it." He grinned. "I've thought about it for a long time, and honestly I think we'd be good for each other."

"How do you figure?" she stuttered.

"It's just," he said as their limousine pulled to the curb of the airport, "you take good care of me. Without you, I'd still be playing in bars and doing God knows what with my spare time. I'd probably be a drunken bastard right now."

As they walked to their gate, she imagined what it'd be like married to him. At first, it'd probably be interesting. Then there'd be other women, nights alone while he was off drinking with the guys.

She shuddered at the thought as they sat down in their first class seats. It wasn't exactly an image she wanted to hold in her mind for the fifteen-hour flight to New York.

"I'm going to go change before we leave the ground," Morgan told him as she stood up. She unlatched the door on the overhead cabinet and took out her bag.

She pulled out a pair of black slacks and a white long sleeve shirt and headed toward the bathroom in the back. Glad to see it wasn't occupied, she walked inside and shut the door.

First-class bathrooms were so much nicer and roomier than coach stalls she thought as she slipped her clothes off and hung them on the hook attached to the door. Sliding on her slacks, she smiled at the fragrance the flowers on the sink were omitting into the air.

Taking one last look in the mirror as she bunched up her hair, she felt more comfortable. She unhooked her clothes and opened the bathroom door.

As she stepped out, the plane began to move, giving a quick rattling jerk. She lost her footing and dropped her things on the floor and someone caught her before she could fall down.

"Woops. Be careful."

Strong arms held her around her waist, steadying her balance as the plane taxied down the runway. She straightened herself up with the hanging curtain and turned around.

"Thank you," she said, but the man had already made his way into the bathroom.

On her way back to her seat, she caught a familiar scent. It was the same cologne Vince had always used. Cursing the fact she would have to deal with it for the long flight, she made her way back to Sam who was eyeing a gorgeous blond in the seat next to theirs.

Marriage, yeah right, she thought as she stuffed her skirt and blouse into her bag. Standing in the aisle, she fought with the stuck zipper until it finally closed up tight.

As she lifted the bag to the overhead cabinet, someone bumped into her, nearly knocking her down. It was the same man who had caught her near the bathroom, the same one wearing the cologne.

"I'm sorry. Here let me help you." The man reached over her and helped her with her bag, latching the cabinet tight.

His voice was familiar, but she refused to turn around. Vince couldn't possibly be on the same flight she was on, let alone flying from London of all places.

"Thank you." She turned around, but he was already sitting down with his head turned towards the blond bubbly bombshell beside him. The man's hair was shaved so it definitely wasn't Vince.

Morgan sat down and turned to Sam who had already fallen asleep. He had a pillow between him and the window and she wondered if he really meant what he said.

Taking out a magazine from the pouch in front of her, she crossed her legs and thumbed through the pages.

Morgan turned to the next page, trying to ignore the whispers from the couple beside them. Every once in a while, she would hear the woman laugh and it would distract her. She turned a few more pages and then stuffed it back down in the pouch.

She leaned her head down on Sam's arm, looping her arm through his. The warmth of his body was so welcoming she closed her eyes and fell asleep.

She felt like she'd only been asleep for a few moments when she felt someone tapping her arm. It was a marvelous dream she was having. Skiing perfectly down the white snowy slope near the lodge with Vince right with her smiling was an exciting sensation. It ended too soon.

"Hey, wake up," Sam whispered, elbowing her.

Yawning, Morgan opened her eyes. Two steaming plates of shrimp pasta were being served to them on a tray.

"So tell me," Sam asked between bites, "have you thought anymore about what I asked?"

She choked slightly on a piece of pasta. "Actually I have." She wiped her chin with her napkin and smiled. "I really don't think you're ready for marriage, Sam."

He grinned nervously. "So are you telling me your answer is no?"

"I suppose," she answered.

She couldn't wait for Sally's wedding. Sally had called at least a dozen times to make sure she didn't miss her flight.

Morgan took off her earphones and enjoyed the quietness as

she watched the movie. Every once in a while the blond woman would laugh, most likely at something from the movie that didn't seem that funny. Curious at what the woman was laughing about, she glanced over at the couple.

It was immediate.

Her jaw dropped open as if she had been punched in the gut and strung up by her toes until the blood rushed to her head. It was Vince.

Turning her head away from him, she burst out into a short scream, not meaning to. It just came out, startling the entire cabin of people including Sam.

"What's wrong?" he asked, seeing her horrified expression across her whitened face. "You look like you've just seen a ghost."

Morgan glanced up at him with blurring vision. *This can't be happening,* she thought. It had been her imagination. She glanced back at Vince. Yep. It was definitely him.

He was there but awake now and wondering what the commotion was all about.

"I'm not feeling too well. Going to the bathroom," Morgan said fast, grinning nervously as she stepped backwards so Vince wouldn't notice it was her.

"Are you okay?" Sam asked again.

"Fine, I'm fine. It was probably just the pasta didn't settle well. I'll be back."

Morgan couldn't walk. She ran back towards the bathroom hoping she was getting a clean getaway. Wondering what she was going to do, she began to pace the small cove near the bathroom.

•

Vince picked up a magazine and opened it. He tried to ignore the commotion as he began reading an article about cooking.

"Oh my God." The blond he was with elbowed him, making him drop half of the magazine from his hand.

Vince glanced at her and noticed she was staring across the aisle at someone. "What?"

"Do you know who that is?" She bounced up and down in her

seat with an excited squeal. "That's the lead singer from Triton. He's sitting right across from me!"

Her eyes grew wide, but Vince's grew twice as big. That meant—he twisted his head quickly to look back—the woman who ran back to the bathroom was Morgan.

Ignoring her squeals, Vince got up hiding his face from Sam as he sauntered towards the bathroom. He ignored stares from the angry passengers being disturbed as he knocked on the bathroom door and leaned in to it.

"Morgan, I know it's you," he whispered loudly, waiting a moment for a response, but she didn't come out. "Open the door, Morgan."

He knocked again, and this time the door slowly opened. Vince gasped, hoping to see Morgan's face, but was knocked back as a large elderly lady came out with a scowl. She glared at him hatefully as she passed.

"I'm sorry, ma'am." He grinned innocently as the scolding woman made her way to her seat.

He glanced around. Opening the blue curtains to the coach section, he searched the uncomfortable passengers, but there was nobody who resembled her. Sighing, he sat down on the stewardess bench with his hands in his face, rubbing his jaw. She couldn't hide for the rest of the flight.

Deciding to head back to his seat, he stood up. But after his first step, he noticed the curtain beside the bathroom was moving slightly, and it was bulged just enough to show an outline of someone hiding behind it.

Glancing down, he noticed someone's two bare feet sticking out at the bottom. She wiggled her painted red toes hoping she wouldn't be caught.

Vince couldn't help but grin. "Well, I guess I'll go back to my seat then. It was just my imagination." Pretending to leave, he stomped his feet from loud to soft until Morgan finally peeked from behind the curtain.

"Caught you." He grabbed her by the wrist and pulled her into the bathroom with him. He shut the door behind them and turned to face her.

"What are you doing here?" She tried to keep her voice down.

"I was about to ask you the same question." He smirked, letting go of her wrist.

"I'm traveling with my fiancé." She stuck her nose in the air and folded her arms.

"Fiancé?" He stepped back on his heel to keep his balance.

"Yeah, Sam asked me to marry him."

"I know," he returned stubbornly.

"You know?"

"Yeah." He threw her a puzzled look.

She refused to look at him, or was more afraid she might lose herself in his eyes. "Why are you on this flight?"

"I'm coming back from a competition."

She softened her face as she returned her gaze to him. "Did you win?"

"Yeah, it was great. You should've seen my performance. I don't think I've ever done that well before at a comp—" His voice trailed as he realized he was being a bit too relaxed.

"What did you do to your hair?" she asked.

"I shaved it. Do you like it?"

"It looks good."

After a moment of silence, she cleared her throat nervously. "So, is that your new manager out there?"

"Yeah, that's Sherrie. She's great. We're getting married this summer," he stuttered nervously. "Possibly, maybe next winter we could."

Her heart sank, but she quickly recovered with a stern eye when she saw he was lying. "Well, if you want to go for the trampy, blond type, then I'm happy for you," she said, going along with it. "Good luck with that."

She went for the door to escape, but he caught her by the arm. He swung her back around to face him.

"Damn it, Morgan." He sighed. "I've missed you."

She wanted to jump into his arms, but fought the urge. She

screamed under her breath. "You've got some nerve to say that when we have nothing else to say to each other. You made it clear you didn't want anything to do with me."

"That's not true," he argued. "Sam told me you wanted to go with him and you two were going to get married."

"He lied to you, Vince," she replied. "He wanted two months of my time and then I'd be free to come back to you, but I wasn't going to take his offer."

"Well, whatever the story is, you left me."

"You forced me to leave," she snapped at him angrily.

"I never forced you to do anything. But I obviously don't want someone that sleeps with every guy she sees."

"What are you talking about?"

"I know you slept with Max that night he left you on the mountain. I knew something had happened by the strange way you were acting."

"I never slept with him."

"You don't have to lie about it."

"You don't believe me?" Tears of anger blurred her vision.

"Morgan," he continued, "just admit it so we can move on and maybe I'll forgive you for it, unless you don't want me to. Maybe Sam's money is just too good to pass up. If I were him, I'd make you sign a pre-nuptial agreement."

She gave a loud huff through her teeth and stormed out of the bathroom door. She made her way back to her seat feeling as though she were going to explode.

Sam was sound asleep, which was a good thing otherwise he'd see her start to cry. Tired, aggravated and frustrated, she closed her eyes. She wiped tears from her cheeks every so often until they finally dried. But just as she fell asleep, the cabin lights came on.

She was glad it was over. Hoping she wouldn't have to see him again, she hurried her and Sam out of the plane and to the long black limousine that waited for them outside to take them to the church.

•

The wedding was absolutely beautiful. Sally made such a lovely bride. With her face glowing, she was the image of a dark haired beauty from a bridal magazine. Laced with white pearls around the neckline, straps made of silk over her shoulders, and a five-foot train that dragged the floor behind her, the dress was made for a princess.

Everyone in the movie industry was there, it seemed. Five hundred glamorous people packed inside the large cathedral church, talking about new films they were starring in, directing or auditioning for.

With Sam at her side, he too had indulged in shaking hands with some of the superstars who recognized him. Some even claimed Triton was their favorite band, which was a proud moment for him.

The reception was just as extravagant. With a seven-layer white cake decorated in lavender streams that dipped down on the sides to small roses of the same color, it was marvelous. Morgan couldn't imagine how difficult it had been for them to put it together.

Champagne glasses were stacked up in a pyramid and gave the illusion of a fountain glittering under the lights. A long table was set with bowls of nuts, mints and finger foods, including caviar and imported crackers she thought were absolutely divine.

Morgan watched in humor as Sally and Kurt both stuffed cake into each others mouth, doing the usual messy smear around the lips. Everyone in the room laughed. Given it was a cliché moment, it was still amusing to watch.

After the reception had gone on for over an hour, Morgan found herself sitting alone at a table, eating honey-glazed chicken that was served as dinner.

"I'm so glad you came." Sally sat down in the chair beside her with the biggest grin she had ever seen her wear.

After a long hug, Morgan set her fork down and smiled. "I envy you. You look so happy."

"I am." She laughed. "I've been meaning to catch up to you so we can talk for quite some time now." Sally took her by the hand. "But my life has been one adventure after another these days. How is everything going with you? How's the tour?"

"It's good." Morgan picked up her fork and played with the remains of the chicken on her plate.

"You look awful."

Morgan twisted her lips. "Thanks a lot, Sal. I did just spend the past fifteen hours on a plane, so yeah, I'm a little worn out."

"It's more than that. What's wrong?"

"There's nothing wrong," she lied. Just like Sally to see right through her.

"You're not still thinking of Vince are you?"

"That's the question of the year," Morgan mumbled. "I saw him on the plane with his new manager."

"Oh, I bet that was awkward." Sally took a sip from her glass.

Morgan nodded. "I thought for sure we were going to mend things, but somehow he has this crazy idea I slept with Max, and he wants to forgive me for it."

Sally lowered her brows in thought. "You didn't sleep with Max, did you?"

"No. He said Sam told him I did, but I've never said anything to him about Max."

"Then what's the problem?" Sally asked happily. "If everything's forgiven, then get over the hurdle. Be forgiven if it makes him feel any better, and then move on."

"Easier said than done." Morgan shrugged.

Sally said, "My mother always told me love is the key to living a full and happy life. Without it, we'll just amble through without a cause. Honestly, I believe our main purpose in life is to spread love around regardless of the toils involved. It's better to be loved than to hold a grudge."

"Spread love around," she repeated. "That sounds like something a hippy would say."

"Well, life is short. Have fun and stop worrying about finding the right man. You're still young. There's plenty of time to find him." Sally smiled.

•

After the wedding was over, Morgan and Sam walked up the sidewalk to her front door. Another one of her plants had died. Noticing the green leaves of her young potted cypress tree had turned a shriveled brown, she sighed. Another one of her favorite plants. Dead.

She unlocked the front door and went inside the house. The sudden image of the night she spent with Vince not long ago invaded her mind. Everything seemed to send memories of him rushing through her all at once. Knowing she had to push away her emotions, she kicked her shoes off in the middle of the floor and frowned.

"Our flight leaves at eleven tonight," Sam reminded her as he grabbed a beer out of the refrigerator. "Only another month of being overseas, and then we can start the American tour."

Morgan picked up another dead plant and carried it to the garbage can. Emotions of sadness crept over her as she set it inside. She tried to fight it, but she didn't have the strength to do it anymore. Bursting into tears, she fell to her knees, put her face in her hands and cried.

"What's wrong?" Sam asked from the kitchen. "I never figured you as such an avid environmentalist to mourn over one small tree."

She couldn't stop crying. Sam was too ignorant to understand it wasn't the tree she was upset over. Straightening herself up, she wiped tears off her cheeks with the back of her hand.

"Oh, Sam." She laughed, trying to keep herself from bursting into another fit of tears. "I'm just tired. Can we stay here tonight and leave tomorrow instead?"

Sam pondered for a moment and immediately unsheathed his cell phone from its case on his belt. Setting the beer bottle down on the counter, he dialed a number and started to talk.

Morgan knew he was calling his other manager to change the flight for the next day. Usually he'd call her and have her do something like that, but lately she'd been more of his ornament rather than a manager.

Sam ended his call with a grin. "Okay, it's set." He walked over to her and pulled her up to her feet. "We're not leaving until tomorrow morning."

Morgan sniffled and smiled. "Thanks."

He pushed her hair over her shoulders and heaved a sigh. "I'd do anything for you. You know that don't you?"

She nodded wrapping her arms around his waist. "I know."

"I've been thinking." He took her hands into his, and looked into her eyes. "Maybe you should stay here for the rest of the tour."

"Why would you say that?"

He pulled her with him to the living room and sat down on the arm of the couch. With her in front of him, he stared up into her eyes.

"Take some time and go to my house. Gain control over these sweeping emotions you have. Relax. Ride some horses. Swim in the pool. Go Christmas shopping or whatever you want to do. Take a vacation and just think again about giving us a try. You're obviously still crying over him and it makes me jealous."

"I'm not crying over anyone, Sam."

He curved his lips into a concerned grin. "You can't fool me. Just think about it overnight and let me know before I have to leave tomorrow."

Chapter 13

"I love it when you bring me here." Sherrie practically danced through the front door of Joe's Bar with Vince straggling behind her, yawning. "I hope you don't mind if I drink a little tonight."

"Knock yourself out." Vince followed her to the bar and sat down in the stool beside her.

Her teeth showed brilliantly as she awed at the Christmas decorations hanging around the room. He wondered where she got all of her energy and wished he had just as much. She was only four years younger than he was, so it couldn't be much of an age thing. He was an athlete—physically fit, healthy and lively, yet she never seemed to stop. Life was like one big party to her and it was never-ending.

"You look tired." She smiled at him when he leaned his chin on his fist and closed his eyes. "Come on, tomorrow's Christmas Eve. We have a lot to celebrate!"

"We just got back from England a few days ago," Vince mumbled. "I think I've only had a few hours of sleep since."

"I'm going to go dance." Sherrie popped off her seat. Armed with a smile she eyed a man dressed in a green Oregon Ducks jersey who was smiling back at her.

"Okay." Vince opened his eyes and started watching a basketball game on the plasma TV on the wall in front of him.

"I haven't seen you in a while," Jim said from behind the bar. "What can I get you?"

"A beer is fine, Jim," he incoherently muttered.

"Whoa. You look like you've just lost your best friend." He popped the cap off the bottle and set it down in front of him. "Want to talk about it?"

Vince eyed him and chuckled. "Not really."

Jim shrugged with a grin and wiped down the counter with a white soapy rag. "In all the years you've been coming here, I've never seen you drag yourself across the floor like that."

He laughed. Jim was right. He'd never felt so bad in his life, although he couldn't quite figure out why. He should feel good about himself after winning an international competition.

Sponsors had been picking him back up again. He had already been invited to compete at another in Washington State after the Olympics, making it his final match of the winter season. So what was wrong with him? How come he couldn't enjoy his life now?

Morgan. It was all her fault.

Even though the thought crossed his mind she'd been telling him the truth from the start, he still couldn't trust her or any other woman for that matter, especially when it came to Max.

He tried to push her from his mind and keep his attention on the basketball game on TV. Someone in the stands was wearing a navy blue Yankees sweatshirt cheering. It reminded him of Morgan so much it hurt.

He found Sherrie dancing quite provocatively on the dance floor. He pulled her out by her arm. "Can you take a cab back when you're done? I'm leaving."

"Where are you going?" she whined, continuing her dance with him. She rubbed her backside against him pulling her long blond hair up to the top of her head and then letting the strands go in his face.

"I'm going for a ride."

Leaving fast so he wouldn't hear her whine again, he pulled the key to his motorcycle from his pocket. He knew exactly where he wanted to go. He had to see Morgan and find out if she was really going to marry Sam. One look in her eyes and he'd know for sure.

As he started up his motorcycle, the thought of her marrying someone else made him cringe. There was no way he'd allow it, no matter what he had to do to stop it.

He thought about her the entire way to her house. Driving through the lit streets of the city, stopping at every red light, he couldn't imagine losing her to anyone.

It wasn't until he finally turned into her subdivision did his breath quicken at the thought of seeing her. The lights were on in her house and he knew she was home.

He parked on the opposite side of the street and turned off his motorcycle. Afraid to go knock on the door, he sat there for a long time debating if he should or not. What if Sam was there?

As soon as he decided to do it, the lights in the house went off. He felt like beating down the door, but instead he gave up. It was the best thing to do now. Leave her alone and let her try to be happy with a man that he knew couldn't be faithful to her.

As he walked back to his motorcycle, a taxi pulled up into her driveway and honked. When he saw her, his heart leapt into his throat. She rolled two large suitcases down the steps to the cab and got in.

Curious where she was going, he started up his motorcycle and followed her cab out onto the main highway. Feeling a little guilty for spying on her, he wondered if he should turn the other way and go home, but he couldn't bring himself to do it.

He followed her all the way to the airport. Parking his motorcycle on the curb, he followed her inside the terminal and to the ticket counter. Figuring she was going back to work with Sam, he knew he had to stop her and talk to her. But as he was about to call out her name, he noticed she had stepped in a line that wasn't international.

Keeping his distance by letting two people in front of him, the curiosity of where she was actually going inspired him to keep up his chase. He picked up a brochure from the booth and held it to his face just in case she glanced back.

"Excuse me, sir." A woman standing behind him smiled. "Are you going to Chicago, too?"

Vince hoped her thick New York nasal accent wouldn't catch Morgan's attention. Nodding with a grin, he answered without saying a word.

He eyed Morgan in hopes she wouldn't turn around from the annoying voice behind him, but she did. He quickly covered his face with the brochure and held his breath. Luckily, the line moved up and she faced forward again before she saw him.

When she finally reached the counter, he was about to go insane. He could barely hear where she was flying to over the woman behind him now talking about the blind date she had the night before.

"Chicago," he heard her say. What was she going to Chicago for? He knew there was only one way to find out, and that was to fly there too.

Watching her leave to go catch the flight, he desperately wanted to stop her, but for some reason he was having too much fun. In a way, he felt like he was a secret agent following his suspect in hopes he'd catch them for a crime they committed.

He'd interrogate her until she confessed. And the crime? That she wasn't in love with the man she had been paid to marry. She'd slept with another man while they were together.

Vince purchased a ticket and hoped he wasn't going to be assigned to the seat next to hers. He hadn't even thought of that as he walked nervously towards the gate. Asking himself what he was doing, he almost tossed the ticket in the garbage and turned around to leave.

It was ridiculous to be going after her anyway, he thought, as he walked down the ramp to board the plane. He shouldn't be going after her. She should be going after him. After all, she was the one who ruined everything to begin with.

Sneering at the thought, Vince stopped at the bottom of the ramp. He was bumped into twice and tossed glares from a few people trying to get by, but it didn't matter to him. As he looked down at his ticket, he debated.

Go and find out, believe in her, mend the relationship and forget everything that had happened? Or should he just turn around and forget about her, let her marry the jerk who thinks he can buy her love?

"Sir, are you boarding now?" A stewardess stood in the doorway of the plane with a smug smile. "If you aren't, you're going to have to leave the boarding ramp."

Vince sighed, unsure he was making the right decision as he stepped inside the plane. He hadn't planned on going anywhere and knew security would impound his motorcycle still parked on the curb.

A fine would need to be paid, but for some reason it didn't matter. It was a small price as he found his way to his seat, covering his face with the brochure.

His seat was all the way in the back, luckily behind Morgan. As he sat down, he wondered why he couldn't just face her. Remembering their meeting on the plane just a few days ago, he didn't think it'd be a good idea to let her know he was there, too. She'd probably be mad at him for following her. And in coach seats, it'd definitely be a bad idea to start an argument there.

He watched her during the entire flight.

When the plane finally landed at Chicago O'Hare, he followed her to the bag return and waited near the exit.

With the brochure still in his face, he held his breath as she walked right by him. She went outside and hopped into the back of a white Lincoln Towncar that had obviously been waiting for her.

As the driver tucked her bags inside the trunk, Vince scrambled to find a cab. He had come too far to lose sight of her now.

He hopped into the back seat of a bright yellow cab with a sigh of relief to the large, rather hairy driver who stared at him in the rearview mirror. He eyed him suspiciously.

"Where to?" the cab driver asked.

"Just follow the white car in front of you." Vince pointed as the car inched out into the traffic of leaving city busses and cabs.

"What are you, a detective?" The man grunted with a smirk.

"No. I just want you to follow it." He glanced at his name tag on the dashboard. "Just follow the car, Pete."

"Listen, if you're some kind of stalker going after your next victim, I'm not taking you anywhere near that woman who got inside." Jim folded his arms. "As a matter of fact I'm not going to take you anywhere."

Vince knew he had to get him to move, and the only thing he could think of was money. "I'll pay you triple the cab fare if you move now."

Pete immediately put the car into gear and pulled out in front of a bus nearly missing it by inches. "You got it."

Vince glanced up ahead and spotted the white car pulling out onto the exit ramp. "Can you go a little faster?"

"Sure. Let me put the car into fly mode and we'll take to flight over the buses."

Vince rolled his eyes, aggravated Morgan was getting away and his rude obnoxious driver was letting it happen. "Just go."

As soon as they hit the interstate, Vince was happy to see the car right in front of them. He wanted desperately to be with her, but instead was incognito with some fat hairy jerk who wouldn't stop asking him questions.

"So where are you going anyway?" Pete asked sucking on the end of a cigar that stunk up the cab.

"I don't know," Vince replied. "You mind rolling down your window a little?"

Pete eyed him and slightly cracked the window. "You know it's thirty-five degrees outside."

Ignoring him, Vince noticed the traffic had thinned remarkably as they pulled off the interstate and onto a dark highway. Snow blanketed the shoulder of the road, and he wondered how much longer they were going to drive.

"Listen, maybe you should back off a distance. I don't want her to think she's being followed."

"Sure thing, boss," Pete chuckled then pulled over to the side of the road and stopped. Silence filled the car as he waited until she was far ahead and then pulled back out onto the road.

"Thanks." Vince grinned watching as the cars brake lights glowed red. It was stopping. The road turned into a gated driveway and the car sped up the hill with the gates closing behind them.

"Want me to pull in?" Pete asked as they neared the turnoff.

"No." Vince sighed. "Just take me back to the airport."

"Okay." Rolling his eyes, Pete turned the cab around and headed back up the road.

Taking out his cell phone, he stared at her number in his contact list. He wanted to delete it, but somehow he couldn't bring himself to.

"Call her." Pete said glancing back at him in the mirror. "I've seen many men drive themselves crazy over a woman, but they're too stubborn to admit they're in love with her."

Vince chuckled and tucked his cell phone back inside his pocket. "I can't call her."

"Why not?" Pete asked with a huff. "If I hadn't called my wife, I'd be a lonely old fool right now."

"She's getting married."

Vince stared out the window into the darkness of the woods thinking what an idiot he was for letting her get off the plane with Sam. If he'd just kept his mouth shut and trusted her. It was obvious he should. She'd never lied to him before about anything else.

"There's no ring on her finger yet is there?" Pete lit up another cigar as they merged into the traffic on the interstate. "It sounds easy enough to me, especially if you believe she's in love with you."

Vince wondered where this driver came from. He imagined cab drivers had a lot of adventures during their rides. Maybe they even retained enough information to become therapists.

"It's not that simple." He glanced over at the city lights as they drove towards the airport.

"Nothing in life is simple."

Vince thought for a moment, staring at his cell phone. What Pete said was true. And if it meant he'd have to fight Sam for her, he'd do it.

"Wait."

"Change your mind?" Pete asked as he suddenly pulled over to the shoulder and stopped the car.

"It's too late to take a flight out tonight, so get off at the nearest hotel. I think I'll be staying the night."

"The man finds his balls." Pete grinned as he pulled back onto the interstate and drove to the next exit.

Chapter 14

Morgan hopped up onto the horse like a professional. She had never ridden one before in her life, and the caretaker was leery about saddling up Sam's proud and quite aggressive black stallion for her. Insisting she was going to be fine, she'd begged him to help her.

Thinking it would be smooth and easy, she hit the horse in the ribs with her heels and he took off fast, too fast. With the horse snorting loudly over his thundering hooves, she held onto the reigns tight as she violently bounced to the side. Luckily she stopped him just before she fell on the ground with a loud thud.

Trying to catch her breath, she stood up and leaned over with her hands on her knees. "Damn. Not what I expected."

Grabbing the horses reigns, she walked him back to the stables. She handed him to the caretaker who shot her an I-told-you-so glance.

"I don't want to hear it." She laughed and then headed up the path to the house dusting off her clothes.

When she walked inside the mud room, she took off her boots and realized her phone was ringing. Much to her pleasant surprise, it was a soft voice she hadn't heard in such a long time.

"Regina, how are you?" Morgan squealed in excitement.

"Hey, Morgan." Regina's voice smiled brightly. "I'm doing wonderful. How are you?"

"I'm good. It's kind of lonely in this big house by myself, but it's been nice."

"I'm having a New Year's Eve party here at my mother's house," Regina said. "I want you to come."

"It sounds like fun, but I doubt I can make it."

"Emma's going to be here."

Morgan ran some cold water inside the cup and stuck it in the microwave. "Emma? I didn't know you were acquainted with her."

Regina sighed. "While you were at the lodge, Emma and Chad came into the office to sign some papers for the junior event." She laughed nervously. "Chad and I really hit it off, so now we're engaged."

"Engaged?" she said in shock as she pulled the hot cup out of the microwave and ripped open a tea packet. She dangled it in the water with a raised brow.

"Yeah," she laughed.

"But you've only known him for what, a month?"

"Yeah," Regina laughed again. "Isn't it crazy?"

A long silence filled the room, giving it a sense of tension as the name rolled around in Morgan's head. She couldn't believe it.

"I guess I'm happy for you, but are you sure you're doing the right thing? Shouldn't you wait a little while before you jump into marriage?"

"Hey," she complained, "I'm not telling you how much of a mistake you're making, so don't talk to me about doing the right thing."

Regina sighed. "You know Sam called last month."

"What?" Morgan was shocked to hear it.

"Yeah," Regina continued. "He asked how he could find you. He said it was urgent, so I told him you were at the lodge. I'm sorry I did that now."

A thought crossed her mind. Hoping she was wrong about it, she rolled her eyes to the ceiling and sighed.

"You wouldn't have told him about what Max did to me?"

The long pause said it all. She could hear Regina breathe with a few cursing whispers to herself.

"I'm so sorry, Morgan," Regina pleaded. "I had no idea Sam would use that information against you."

"It's okay," Morgan said. "It's not your fault."

"I'm sorry. Come to Seattle for New Year's. It's going to be quite a party. I'm sure Emma would be happy to see you one more time before you get married. Come on. It'll be fun."

Morgan shrugged. "I'll let you know."

The gate intercom beeped, startling her slightly. She buzzed whoever it was in. Most likely it was the crew that cleaned the horse stalls, though they weren't supposed to be there until after Christmas day.

After a few minutes the doorbell rang. She clipped her hair up and swung the door open expecting to hand out the key to the shed. But she gasped when she saw Vince standing before her. He held two small wrapped boxes in one hand and a birthday cake in the other.

"What are you doing here?" Her heart leapt to her throat.

"Happy birthday," he said, glancing past her as if looking for someone else.

"I'm right here," she puckered her lips and squinted her eyes.

"Are you alone?" he asked in a whispering voice.

"Yes," she answered stepping back from the doorway. "Come in before you freeze to death."

He handed her the cake as he stepped inside the house. "He has a nice place."

"Take off your shoes," she demanded trying not to let the excitement of seeing him overwhelm her.

She watched him. It was comical to see him taking off his shoes like he was out of his element.

"How did you find me here?" she asked as she led him to the kitchen.

"I followed you from the airport."

"So now you've turned into a stalker." She set the cake down on the counter.

"I had to see you."

"What's your fiancée going to think?"

"Fiancée?" He thought for a moment. "You mean Sherrie? Oh, she's fine with it."

"It's Christmas Eve. Why aren't you home spending it with your family?" she asked as she stood nervously, back against the counter.

"Honestly," he said as he moved towards her, eyeing her intently. "I knew you were by yourself. I didn't want you to spend the holidays alone."

She inspected his face. The shadow on his jaw had grown into a short-stubble beard and she could tell he hadn't slept by the dark circles under his eyes.

"What happened to you?" she asked, avoiding getting boxed in by suddenly moving. "You look awful." She found the tea kettle on the stove and began filling it with water.

"Thanks," he replied. The cynical tone in his voice was prominent. "Let's see," he continued with a frown as he leaned back against the counter. "I've spent the last few weeks with one of the most annoying women I've ever met because the woman that I hired left me to make more money. And I spent the past few days chasing after her even though she's marrying another guy." He shook his head with a glare. "I don't know what the hell I'm doing here."

She watched him as he sauntered off towards the front door. Her eyes grew wide in aggravation, shock and total fear if she let him leave now, he'd be gone forever.

She eyed the small round cake he brought for her. It was decorated with pink hearts and a ribbon edging that matched the writing. "Happy birthday, Morgan," she read aloud.

"Wait!" she yelled as she ran through the kitchen and great room toward the door.

She found her shoes on the mat beside the wall and grabbed one. Seeing it was untied, she slipped her foot inside easily. The other shoe gave her problems. As she tried to put it on without loosening the laces, she stumbled. Hopping around on one foot, she tried to catch her balance, but failed.

With a miserably shocking groan, she fell back on the floor. The painful blow to her backside made her lie back with her hands to her sides and stare at the ceiling, wishing to God she wasn't so clumsy.

"That looked like it hurt," Vince said, chuckling as he came to stand overtop of her.

Without moving her eyes to him, she pursed her lips. "I must look like an idiot right now."

"Maybe a little." He laughed as he offered her his hand.

"I thought you were leaving."

"I was," he said as he pulled her up to her feet. "I had to call a cab."

She looked at the phone in the living room. He'd been standing there the entire time, watching her make a fool out of herself. She suddenly blushed.

"Did you call them yet?" she stuttered slightly as she cleared her throat, tilting her head.

"No."

"Well," she continued, "I can't eat that cake by myself. Stay and have a piece with me?"

"I don't know," he folded his arms over his chest. "Do you think we can be civil to each other long enough to eat it?"

"Possibly." She nodded. "I mean, we could have dinner first."

"Dinner? That means I'd have to spend the day here."

"It's okay." She sighed. "You can leave if you like. I just thought maybe, since you're here—"

"Okay, dinner sounds good," he said. His grin turned to a frown as he rubbed his jaw. "I could really use a shave though. I went off and left everything at home."

"I have an extra razor," she said. "It's a woman's razor, but I'm sure it'll work fine."

He cringed. "I don't know. I've never used one before." He touched her lightly on the arm. "Maybe you should do it for me."

She gazed up into his emerald stare. The serious glance he gave her made her tremble, an incredibly delightful sensation.

"Fine," she agreed to his strange request. "I'll meet you in the kitchen."

She went upstairs and gathered the things she needed. As she made her way back down the stairs, she glanced in the large round mirror on the wall and stopped.

"What am I doing?" she asked herself under her breath as she continued her walk to the kitchen.

She shouldn't have allowed him to come in. After all the heartache and annoyance she'd been through with him, she was acting like everything was okay, when it clearly wasn't.

She walked through the doorway to the kitchen and immediately stopped. Her skin rose as she watched him, sitting quietly in the middle of the kitchen. His shirt was off. His toned body seemed to attract the light, beautifully spotlighting him like he was a decoration in the room.

How was she going to make it through this? she thought miserably as she set the shaving pot, cream and the razor down on the table.

He watched her intently as she applied the cream to his face. It was distracting in a sense she was going to have a hard time keeping her concentration on the task.

She touched the razor to his skin and slowly pulled it up over his jaw. "I've never shaved anyone's face before," she admitted.

He eyed her intently as she rinsed off the darkened cream from the blade in the pot of warm water.

"You're staring," she said.

"Does that bother you?"

"No," she confessed, "but tell me what's on your mind." She pulled the razor up again.

"I believe you."

"Believe me?"

"I should've believed you when you first told me you hadn't slept with him, but I was too stubborn to listen."

Morgan hesitated before she rinsed out the razor again realizing he was talking about what happened with Max. She tossed him a shushing smile.

"Forget about it. It's in the past."

"I should've trusted you."

"It's okay," she said as she applied another stroke to his face.

"I found my last girlfriend in bed with another guy one night. I guess that's why I have a hard time with trust."

She glanced at him with a frown. "I didn't know that."

"That's why I believed you'd done the same thing."

"Well," she said, rinsing the razor again. "I guess I would've had the same thoughts if I were you. But, in my own defense, you should've known I was telling you the truth. After all, our relationship is supposed to be based on honesty and disclosure."

He chuckled. "Even now you're all business."

"Sorry." She gave out a short laugh through her nose.

"Your eyes are gray." He enjoyed her touch as she held his chin and ran the razor down the side of his face. "You're sad when they turn that color."

"Hold still." She scolded when he tilted his head to the side.

He held his head rigid, trying not to grin. "You're still beautiful."

"And you look handsome again." She smiled, finishing the last stroke.

He stood up and wiped his face with the towel. Feeling awkward, she turned from him and took the pan to the sink, hoping he wouldn't follow her. But he was already treading her way and slowly closing in.

"I feel a lot better." He rubbed his smooth face with his hand. "Maybe I should hire you to do this for me all the time."

She laughed nervously as he came to stand behind her. He put his hands on her shoulders, but she moved away quickly.

"Vince."

Sighing, he leaned up against the counter, watching her move the chair back to the table. "You aren't seriously going to marry him. He doesn't deserve you."

"So what do I deserve then? You? You trusted a complete stranger's word over mine. So don't stand there and tell me that you know what I need."

She tried to maneuver around him, but he caught her shoulders before she could pass. He stared down into her eyes with such a stern look it made her lips tremble.

"Morgan," he said, caressing her arms gently.

"What do you want from me?" Tears formed in her eyes but she couldn't bring herself to move away.

"Isn't it obvious?" He pulled her into his arms and held her close, stroking her hair. "It doesn't matter what happened in the past."

His tone was low and soft. She swallowed down her tears and managed to purse her lips and pull away from his embrace.

"It seems every time we try to be together, something always tears us apart. Maybe that's fate telling us to give up and move on."

"I don't believe in leaving my life in the hands of fate," he said. "I'm here with you on your birthday. I want to stay the night and spend Christmas with you. Can't you get it through your thick skull how much I want you?"

"You can't have me anymore, Vince. Remember, you ripped up my contract." She turned around and found her shoes on the floor. Sliding them on her feet she felt his eyes on her. "You're just going to have to accept it's over between us."

She pulled her jacket off the hook of the mud room and walked out the back door. She strolled down to the horse stables and went inside completely flustered that she was, again, making him leave when she didn't want him to at all.

"Get a grip on yourself, Morgan," she whispered leaning over the gate that kept Sam's horse in.

"I'm sorry." Vince walked up behind her and rested his hands on her shoulders. "I wish I could turn back time. I'd fix everything the way it was supposed to work out."

"Maybe you should just leave," she said.

"If that's really what you want, then I will."

"No," she confessed. "It's not what I want."

"Then tell me what you want me to do?"

She turned around and looked him square in the eyes knowing she would regret what she was going to tell him. And after taking a deep breath, she grinned.

"I want you to stay for dinner."

•

"You had a part in a soap opera?" Morgan burst out into hysterics holding her napkin to her face.

"Yeah, Sherrie has a screw loose somewhere."

Taking another sip of wine, she was glad he stayed. "I just can't believe your mom hired her in the first place."

"Well," he took a bite of his steak, "you know she always has ulterior motives."

She grinned. "I wonder what they were when she hired me."

He set his fork down in his plate and leaned back. "My entire life she's been telling me I need a strong woman to keep me out of trouble. So maybe that's what she thought when she heard about you."

Morgan blushed, wishing she hadn't accepted the third glass of wine. She felt relaxed, maybe a little too much for her own good.

"I almost didn't take the job because I've never dealt with an athlete before. It's much easier than dealing with a musician." She chuckled, glancing down at her plate in thought. "Sam, he was definitely a handful. He still is."

"I guess you heard Chad is getting married."

"Yeah, I heard. Regina called me a few days ago." She stood up with her plate in hand. "I think it's a little soon, but I'm happy for them."

"I was shocked when I heard about it. I never thought he would be one for marriage and kids."

She grinned as she made her way to the sink. She suddenly felt his hands on her shoulders. Closing her eyes, she let him massage. It felt wonderful, though she knew she shouldn't let him continue.

"Are you ready for dessert?" he whispered in her ear.

His touch was inviting, passionate in a sense she knew he wasn't talking about the cake on the counter. She turned around to face him and opened her mouth to tell him it couldn't happen, but he interrupted her.

"I need you," he said. "I love you."

"Don't say that," she whispered.

His eyes penetrated hers with a look she'd seen him wear on that glorious day they had together at her house. The day they'd made love for hours. It was the day she wanted to forget, now more than ever.

She let him take her in his arms. The sensation tingling throughout her body was relaxing and comforting as he held her there, stroking her hair.

"You can't tell me you don't feel it, too," he whispered, touching his lips to her ear. "I'm sorry I let you go, but I promise I won't let that happen again."

She shivered, closing her eyes and fighting the arousal she felt from his strong arms around her shoulders. His breath on her ear wasn't helping matters at all.

"You have a lot of nerve coming here." She found the strength to pull away. "You got what you wanted last time, but I'm not falling for your sweet talk just so you can get me in bed again."

"Is that what you think? You think I want to have sex with you?"

"Yes," she said with a quick rise in her voice that would have struck her as funny if the moment wasn't so serious.

He put a finger to his mouth as if he were deep in thought. Then as if a light came on with his answer, he genuinely smiled.

"Ah yes, of course," he said. "I just spent the past day and a half listening to some nasally inclined woman on a plane talk about her dysfunctional family, paid triple cab fare to one of the rudest drivers in Chicago, and risked getting shot at by an overindulgent, possessive spoiled rotten rock star just so I can have sex with you."

"You went through all that just to get here?"

"Yes," he yelled, trying to catch his breath as he glared at her. "Not to mention I had to drive to four grocery stores just to find someone to personalize your birthday cake on Christmas Eve."

It was wrong, completely wrong as she threw her arms around his neck and planted her lips on his. At first he didn't know what to do as he stood stiff-lipped and stunned. But with her persistence, he softened his mouth and relaxed his tense muscles.

With her long slender arms around his neck, he lifted her up on the counter. The passion she felt radiated through her body as he lifted her shirt over her head and tossed it into the floor. He pulled his tank off, exposing his broad chest.

She stared at him for a moment, noting his perfectly rounded pecks. They seemed to beckon her as she slid her fingers lightly over them, making his skin rise with a chill.

He slid his arms around her waist and ran his hands up her back, pressing his lips to her neck as he unclipped her bra. He pulled the straps down over her shoulders and lifted it off of her arms.

She trembled in delight when he pressed his body against hers. He was warm, inviting and beautiful. As his tongue dove into her mouth he massaged her hips, pulling off her pants.

Realizing she was about to have sex in the kitchen, she suddenly felt awkward. To be sitting on the kitchen counter completely naked was something she'd never envisioned before, but here she was. It was strange, yet completely arousing and she couldn't wait to feel the sensation when it finally happened.

As she unbuttoned his jeans, she began to enjoy the bad girl feeling emitting through her. She pulled away from his lips and grinned. She pushed his jeans down over his hips and released him from their confinement. He was hard as she gently pulled on him.

He let his pants fall to his ankles and stepped on them until they were off. She could tell he enjoyed it by the sigh he let loose from his lips.

He buried his head in her chest as he massaged her hips, slowly pulling her towards the edge of the counter. His lips moved across her breast to her arm, generously pulling at her skin on the way.

The heat poured from her body as his hand wandered between her thighs. She sighed in perfect pleasure.

The intensity rose with his lips as he kissed her again, passionate and excitingly. And when she felt she couldn't take it any longer, she pulled herself off the counter and into his arms.

With her legs tight around his waist and her arms around his neck, she held on to him as he quickly pushed inside her. The moment intensified as he backed her against the wall and moved his hips in big thrusts.

She breathed with him, imploring him to move harder, faster. The calendar behind her fell from the wall to the floor. Old colored notes that had been written, reminding her of meetings she had, assignments to set up and concert dates for the tour, floated to his feet.

The cordless phone beside them was knocked off the hook from the force of their bodies. It broke into pieces when it hit the floor, but went unnoticed as they kept their attention on each other.

His body was strong, impeccable. The stamina he had was amazing as he held onto her hips. Sweat beaded his body from the heat of the passion swirling around them.

She believed he could go on forever if she let him, but he'd hit that spot inside her, the one that made her immediately gasp. Panting in an uncontrollable cry, she arched her back, leaning her head on the wall behind her.

The feeling was marvelous and exhausting at the same time. The adrenaline that pumped through her veins seemed to explode into a vigorous stem of long pleasured breaths as he buried his face in her shoulder.

His breath was heavy as he tried to catch it. He clasped his hand in hers as their orgasmic fit settled into playful laughs of enjoyment.

He grinned, holding her there until he was finally able to raise his head. She loved the look in his eyes at that moment. It was of pure bliss, and she imagined she held the same stare for him.

He glanced down at the floor and chuckled at the papers that had fallen. "We made a mess," he said, still breathing as if he'd just run a marathon.

She followed his gaze, smiling in pure ecstasy. "I'll clean it up later."

He tried to move away from her and let her down from the wall, but she held fast. Surprised by her reaction, he walked with her to the counter where it all started and leaned her against it.

"You want to stay like this?" he asked with a half-grin.

She blushed in embarrassment. It was true she didn't want him to put her down, but she imagined he was probably tired from all the stress on his back from holding her up that long.

She released her grip on her legs and arms and he set her down on the floor in front of him. With flushed cheeks, she turned away from him and bent down to pick up her clothes.

As soon as she picked them up, he grabbed her around the waist from behind. He pulled her to him and caressed her shoulders with his hands.

"You are the most beautiful woman I've ever seen," he whispered in her ear. "Let me take you away from here."

"Vince."

She meant to argue with him as she turned her head to the side and looked back into his eyes. He wrapped his arms around her.

"You don't belong here in this house." He kissed her lightly on the lips. "You belong with me."

She couldn't argue with him, at least not with the emotions she was feeling at the moment. She wanted him again in a terrible way. Her body ached for him as he swayed with her, holding her tightly in his arms.

She was glad to feel him harden again as he slid down her backside. And within moments, he bent his knees and slipped in from behind.

It sent her head spinning. The rush of his body against her back was exciting. She'd never made love this way before and it was sending her into an immediate fit of gasps.

With his hands on her breasts, massaging them sensually, an erotic sensation rose in her stomach. She couldn't stop the ache as she lifted her arms over her head and grabbed onto his neck behind her.

She moaned loudly as he pulled on her, lowering his hands to her stomach, her hips, her backside. With his arm around her waist, he rubbed between her thighs making her groan even more.

She loved it. The way he made her feel was sensual, sexual, and she was completely overtaken by him. The way he moved, throwing his hips erotically in various ways was exciting. She couldn't stop the rising urge to clamp down on him and burst into orgasm.

The sensation was so overpowering she couldn't help the little screams escaping from her lips with every moaning breath she took. The experience of this much more physical way of making love exhausted her within minutes of starting. She wished she could've held on longer, but she couldn't.

As she cried out her last moan, she was glad he, too, couldn't hold on any longer. Enjoying every gasp that came from his lips, and every time he called out her name, she grinned mischievously.

As if she were intoxicated, she turned to face him with half-open eyes. Groaning in pure enchantment, she raised her lips to his and kissed him in the most stimulating way she knew how.

She enveloped her tongue with his, leisurely licking as she relaxed her lips. With the smile still there, she pressed them gently against his. Closing her mouth, she slowly pulled away and gazed into his eyes.

He gave a pleasured growl, but suddenly moved his eyes away. With an arched brow he leaned over the counter and picked up the two wrapped packages he'd brought for her.

"You didn't open the gifts I brought."

"You didn't have to get me anything."

"Yes I did."

She carefully untied the glittering red bow and tore at the shining gold paper until it revealed a black box. "What is this?"

"Open it," he said as he gazed down into her eyes.

She pulled the lid of the box off revealing a small black cell phone. "Wow, this is really nice."

"Turn it on," he said.

"What about the other gift?"

She set the phone and box down on the counter and pulled the other present from his grasp. With a keen eye she unwrapped it to reveal another black box, but this one was made with velvet material.

She pulled the lid up slowly. Her eyes grew wide in delight as she stared at the most beautiful thin, gold chained necklace she'd ever seen.

"It's lovely." She smiled as he carefully pulled it out of the box for her.

A small golden snowboard dangled from the chain in front of her eyes. As he held it up, she read the burned-in inscription.

"Morgan," she whispered feeling the tears come to her eyes. "You had it inscribed with my name."

"You told me you could never find your name on anything, so I thought I'd have it done for you."

"Thank you," she said as she turned around and gathered her hair in her hands.

"Come home with me." He clasped the necklace around her neck. "I'll call a cab and we can be out of here in an hour. We can spend our Christmas at the lodge."

"It sounds wonderful, but I can't leave just yet," she said, admiring the charm with a smile.

"Why can't you?" he asked.

"I can't leave until he gets home."

"You're house-sitting?"

"Basically," she replied.

He sighed at the thought. With his arms around her shoulders, she knew he was concocting a plan in that amazing head of his.

"If you can't leave, then we'll just have to spend it here together."

"That's your brilliant plan?" she asked, finding humor in how long it took for him to think of it. "I mean seriously," she continued, seeing his playfully perturbed expression. "I couldn't have thought of that myself."

He quickly grabbed her sides with a huff. "You're so in for it," he said playfully.

She laughed. "That tickles!"

She fought her way out of his arms and backed away from him. She shivered as a draft hit her bare skin on the way up the stairs, but it was also from the way he stared at her.

He stepped up the stairs quickly until she found him back in her arms. He picked her up and glanced down the hallway.

"Where's your room?"

She motioned with a nod. "First door to the right."

He carried her into the room and set her down on her feet.

He led her to the bed. She lay down next to him and leaned her head on his chest. She could hear his heart beating like a drum, putting her to sleep. Too much had happened between them. It was going to take time and a lot of effort to make it work, but he was willing to give it a go. And if he was willing to, then so was she.

•

Morgan woke up to the phone ringing. She slid out of Vince's arms, wrapped her robe around her and ran downstairs to answer it.

"Hello," she said completely out of breath from her sprint.

"Hey gorgeous," Sam's voice boomed back.

"Hey," she said sleepily.

"I'm sorry I woke you up, but I just wanted to let you know I'm on my way home."

Morgan gasped. "I thought you had more concerts to perform."

"I do, but I didn't want you to be alone on Christmas. I'm in flight now, so I should be home by this evening." He sighed. "I can't wait to see you."

She grinned at his sincerity. "I can't wait to see you. We have a lot to talk about."

"I know."

"Could you do me a quick favor?" he asked. "I can't seem to get in touch with my accountant. Get my checkbook off the desk in the study and write out a check for ten-thousand to the Maid's Association in Paris."

"That's an odd charity," she replied.

"Could you just do that for me please? I'll send you the address via e-mail," he said in a perturbed voice.

"Sure." She arched her brows. She'd never heard him raise his voice to her before. "What time should I expect you?"

"I'd say around eight o'clock tonight. Oh, and the Christmas tree is on its way."

"It's on its way?"

"Yeah," he replied. "I went ahead and ordered one to be delivered today. Damn. You know how hard it is to find a tree on Christmas day?"

The checkbook was exactly where he said it would be on the large black mahogany study. She sat down in the large swiveling leather chair and looked for a pen. Opening the drawer, she found one on top of the checkbook's register.

As she was about to close the drawer, a name suddenly popped out at her. Curious, she turned the register around and in shock, stared at it. It was an entry with Vince's name on it. And right beside his name was an amount for one-hundred-thousand dollars.

Raising the register up out of the drawer to make sure she wasn't reading it wrong, she realized it was made out on the same date she had quit and left the lodge. Her eyes grew wide as the truth became evident.

Sam bought her out and Vince willingly accepted it. Trying not to believe what she was looking at, she shut her eyes tightly and then opened them. With a horrified glance, she found the name still there.

"Good morning," Vince said walking into the room with a smile.

Finding her in tears as she stared at him in dismay, he stopped on the other side of the desk. He glanced down at the register she held.

"Wait," he said before she could say anything. "Just let me explain."

"Is it true?" she asked, feeling as if her heart had shattered into pieces. "Did you really accept money from him?"

"If you'll let me explain," he said leaning down on the desk. He tried to touch her hand, but she quickly pulled it away from him.

"Explain what? That you both bought and sold me like I was some sort of slave?"

"No," he said, walking towards her. "It wasn't like that at all."

"Stop," she shouted, holding her hand out to show he needed to keep his distance.

He stopped just before her, grinning slightly. "If you'll let me explain, you'll understand what happened."

"I know what happened," she said in a much calmer voice, but still quite perplexed. "He offered you money for my contract, and you took him up on it believing I wasn't faithful anyway. You might as well get rid of the cheating manager and make a little money on the side."

"Wow, I guess you've got me all figured out then, don't you?"

She watched him turn and walk out the door, shaking his head. Sitting back down in the chair, she put her face in her hands and let go of her tears.

After a few moments, she heard his footsteps. He had his shoes on and was walking down the stairs. She quickly stood up and ran out of the room, finding herself stopping at the top of the stairs as he reached the bottom.

With stern eyes, he turned around and looked at her. A moment passed without a word spoken between the two as they stared at each other. The only sound came from the ticking of the Grandfather clock along the wall, until finally Vince opened his mouth to speak.

"Are you really going to let me walk away without an explanation?"

"Sam's on his way home," she said with a cold stare. It was hard to do, but she managed to keep more tears from forming in her eyes. I told you from the start mixing business with personal was a bad idea. Now you know."

She saw the hurt in his eyes before he turned away from her. "Once I walk out that door, I'm gone. I won't come back."

"Goodbye, Vince."

"Merry Christmas," he replied.

She walked to the end of the hallway and stood at the window. She moved the curtain back and watched him walk down the driveway with his cell phone to his ear, most likely calling for a cab.

Every nerve and muscle in her body numbed, and she fell to her knees sobbing. Uncontrolled tears fell from her eyes creating a small pool on the hardwood floor.

It had happened again. They found their way to each other, but something tore them apart. Regardless of how she felt, there was no way she could forgive him for accepting Sam's money. And regardless of the outcome of being alone, she couldn't forgive Sam for offering it to him.

Chapter 15

Sam walked through the door with open arms. With a red Santa hat on his head, he grunted as he picked Morgan up off the floor and swung her around.

"It's so good to be home."

"Sam, what's wrong with you?"

He rolled his eyes and flipped his hair back. "I'm sorry. I don't know what came over me. I guess I'm just exhausted."

Morgan walked over to him and helped him take off his leather jacket. "Listen, why don't you go upstairs and take a shower. That might relax you a bit."

She emptied two suitcases and separated his black T-shirts from his jeans. Amused that all his clothes were definitely in a musician's taste, she began pulling out his underwear.

They were all white, which made her more amused until she saw something pink at the bottom of the bag. Pulling it out, her eyes widened in disgust. It was a woman's thong and someone had written on the front of it with a black marker.

"To my Sam, remember me. Fawn."

It had been too long since she'd had the feeling, the business woman, and the aggressive go-getter she used to be just a few years before. It was all coming back to her in one sweeping emotion. The impending doom of the weak mind she'd lived with for two years was suddenly, imminently and finally gone from her.

With her strong will returned, she walked up the stairs with the panties draped around her finger. She heard the shower turn off and Sam shouting for her to get up there.

She was definitely on her way to leave.

The bathroom door swung open and Sam stood before her glowering as his wet hair dripped down into the floor. He eyed her closely then raised a man's digital watch up to her face.

"Who the hell does this belong to?"

She grabbed it from his hand. It was Vince's watch, but she wasn't going to let Sam know that just yet.

"No more games, Sam," she said in a calm, cool voice. "I want the truth from you now. You paid Vince for my contract didn't you?"

By the sudden look of guilt in his eyes, she knew the answer. She was hoping the money had been for something else, but there was nothing she could think of that could possibly be an alternative.

"I'm so disappointed," she continued. "Of all the horrible things I've put up with, this is the worst."

Sam shook his head as he slipped his boxers on. He sat down at the edge of the bed and eyed her grimly. With his fingers to his temple, he sighed.

"I'm sorry," he said, shaking his head in disappointment. "If I could take it back, I would. But you have to understand I really needed you at the time."

"You knew about what happened with Max. You used your charming ways to convince Vince I cheated on him." She felt the anger rise with her voice. "You gave him a check for a hundred thousand to buy out my contract and then lied to me about it."

Sam watched her closely as he stood up and wandered to the top drawer of his night stand. He dug through his socks until he found what he was looking for and then turned and walked to her with a look of total defeat.

"Here," he said, holding out a rectangular piece of paper.

She glanced down at it curiously, and then took it from his hands. She turned it over and lifted it up. She gasped in dismay when she saw it was the check he'd written to Vince.

"He gave it right back to me," Sam confessed as he returned to his bed and sat down. "It's true I told him you'd slept with Max, but I really don't think he believed me. He never said a word until I told him you really wanted to come with me overseas and were just afraid to tell him. He was only supposed to act like he was angry to get you to leave, thinking it was what you wanted."

Morgan sat down on the bed in utter awe at what she was hearing. In complete shock that Sam had concocted these horrible tales to get her to go away with him was unbelievable.

"I never wanted your money, Sam."

"I know that." He sighed. "But he didn't."

She glanced down at the watch. "I've already packed my bags. I'm going home."

He looked hurt, but he lightened his face as soon as he saw her start to cry. She couldn't help it as she stared at the watch.

"I didn't mean to hurt you." He put his arms around her and held her.

"I know," she said. "It doesn't matter anymore. What's done is done." She pulled away from his embrace. "One thing I don't get though—why go through all of this just for my help? I'm sure you could've found someone else for the job."

"Oh," he grunted as he stood up and began to pace. "I was hoping you wouldn't ask that."

"Maybe I don't want to know."

"No," he disagreed. "I should tell you."

He took her hands in his and pulled her up to her feet. With a growling overtone, he cleared his throat.

"I kept having these dreams about you." He gave her a half-grin. "Ever since that night we had sex, I haven't been able to get you out of my head."

Morgan sighed in relief. She'd thought for sure it was going to be another horror story, but this one was much better.

"I fell in love with you," he continued.

"You didn't." She laughed.

"I thought I had until we went to Sally's wedding." He groaned. "That scared the hell out of me."

"Why didn't you just tell me the truth?" She grinned as his face softened.

"I was afraid to disappoint you. I didn't want to make matters worse, especially after all the lies I told to get you away from Vince."

"I shouldn't have let myself fall for him.

"Don't ever be sorry about love. Just go to him and tell him your feelings. Tell him it was my fault, but he knows that already." He put his arm around her shoulders. "If it was meant to be, you'll know."

She sniffled. "I don't know what I'm supposed to do now."

"You're supposed to go to the airport and buy a ticket back to New York. Find him and tell him you're in love with him. Then the lucky bastard will take you home, have sex with you, marry you and make lots of babies."

Morgan suddenly laughed. "You're unbelievable."

"Hey, I'm just telling it like it is."

A moment went by.

"Why are you still here?" Sam asked with a shrug. "Shouldn't you be getting your little ass out the door?"

Morgan smiled widely. With an excited move, she leaned over and kissed Sam on the cheek. "I love you, you big nut."

"Yeah, yeah, I love you too." He grinned as he watched her run for the doorway. "I'll call the car for you."

Frantic, she quickly fixed her makeup. The smile she wore matched the emotion she carried. She finally knew what she wanted and wasn't going to let him go, not this time and not ever again. She only hoped it wasn't too late.

When she was finally on the way to the airport, it had started to snow. In the back of the car Sam ordered for her, she pulled out the new cell phone Vince had bought her and turned it on. As she watched the glowing light come on, she read the greeting words aloud.

"You own my heart, Morgan. I'm in love with you. Marry me."

Tears immediately formed in her eyes. Why didn't Vince turn

the phone on for her when he was there?

The fear of calling him subsided as she dialed his cell phone number. It rang five times and went to voice mail.

She hung up without leaving a message, unsure of what to say. It was possible he was out of range, maybe on his way up the mountain to the lodge. Or maybe he'd blocked the number, not wanting to talk to her after she'd said those horrible things to him.

The car pulled up to the curb in front of the terminal. The driver pulled her rolling suitcase out of the trunk and opened the door for her.

"Have a safe trip," he said as he helped her step out of the car.

In no time she was heading towards the ticket counter. On Christmas night, she would've thought the place would be empty, but it was packed with people getting an early start home, beating the mad rush.

As she was about to step in line, her cell phone rang. It was the new one, playing the Happy Birthday song for her. The excitement grew as she pulled it out of her pocket, knowing exactly who it was.

"Vince," she said, trying to hold back the squeal forming in her throat.

"Morgan?" he said, his voice sounded surprised. "I saw you called, but I was in the middle of getting my ticket at the airport and didn't get to it in time."

Her heart started to pound vigorously as she panted for breath. "You're at the airport here in Chicago?" she shouted as she suddenly started looking around for him.

"Yeah," he answered.

"I'm here, too!"

Ignoring the stares from the people watching her jump to see over their heads, she laughed. "I'm getting a ticket back to New York. Where are you?"

"I'm at the security checkpoint."

"No. Turn around and come back," she yelled as she picked

her suitcase up and began to run towards the gates. "I know you didn't accept the money. I'm so sorry I doubted you," she shouted, running past the ticket counter.

"It's okay," he said. "You don't have to apologize. Where are you?"

"Over here!" Morgan raised her cell phone in the air, jumping up and down when she saw him pushing through the crowded lobby near the security gate.

She dropped her suitcase and ran to him, pushing people out of her way until finally she hopped up into his arms. Laughing, crying, and knowing if she never felt this alive again, it wouldn't matter.

He swung her around in his arms and kissed her, sending their audience into a fit of applause. A light-headed sensation rushed through her as he set her down on her feet in front of him.

When he parted from her lips, he gave her an ear to ear grin. "What changed your mind?"

She beamed as she slid her arms around his neck. "I own your heart and I'm not about to let it get away from me, not this time."

"You read the message." He chuckled as he gently touched his forehead to hers. "So are you going to marry me or what?" he asked as he stared lovingly into her eyes.

There was no doubt in her mind what her answer was. She would marry him and spend the rest of her life in front of that roaring fire with the man she loved.

She was exactly where she was supposed to be. She loved him more than anything, and he returned it by giving himself solely to her. And for the first time in her life, she knew she was completely whole as she answered with tears in her eyes.

"Yes, and I'd like strawberry pancakes for breakfast in the morning."

Angela Steed

Born in Seattle, Washington, the author grew up in a small town on the Oregon Coast. After living in Portland, Oregon, she moved to the beautiful Appalachian Mountains of West Virginia where she lives with her husband and two daughters. In addition to being a novelist, Angela is a licensed realtor, freelance writer and computer specialist. *1080 Kiss* is her first published romance novel. She's currently working on her next.

Maya's Gold

A contemporary romance
by Mary Vine
ISBN: 978-0-9793252-4-3

Love and Gold. Mystery and Passion.

All famous mystery author Stanton Black wanted was to leave the flashbulbs of Hollywood behind. Hiding out in the wilds of northeast Oregon seemed like the perfect way to get over an attempt on his life while researching his work. His latest novel would draw on the history of his ancestors and the lore of gold country. Now, all he needed was a suitable tour guide.

Special education teacher Maya Valentine was no tour guide. After the death of her parents, Maya has come home to Salisbury Junction for the summer only to have an ailing friend talk her into escorting Stanton around the area. As a pattern of crime around her and the newfound gold on her property leads to mystery, her relationship with Stanton turns to thoughts of romance. A romance too impossible to consider.

A lush, exotic paranormal romance by Kimberly Adkins

ISBN: 978-0-9793252-3-6

A Darkly Enchanted Artifact.

A Passion to Outlast the Centuries.

Solaus had but one wish of the medallion: to save his dying bride. But when he placed the pendant around his neck, his wish was changed by a malevolent twist of magic that made him Djinn, but also took away the knowledge of what he is and who he used to be. Flung from Ancient Persia into immortality, Solaus has only the memory that he did not save his true love—and nothing more as time begins to pass.

Eager for a fresh start, New York City photographer, Kaitlin Sommers accepts a rare assignment on a deserted island fortress off the coast of Alexandria, Egypt. Surrounded by the shadowy underworld of illegal treasure smuggling, Kaitlin finds herself in the arms of man who seems to spring directly from dreams of her past—a man Fate threatens to tear her away from a second time.

The Medallion of Solaus

"With the penning of this novel, Ms. Adkins is definitely on her way to being the ultimate paranormal princess... THE MEDALLION OF SOLAUS is the type of tale true love and legends are spun from—timeless and magically beautiful."

Janalee Ruschhaupt
Paranormal Romance (PNR) Reviews

www.ingramcontent.com/pod-product-compliance
Lightning Source LLC
La Vergne TN
LVHW090940080826
845145LV00003B/824

* 9 7 8 0 9 7 9 3 2 5 2 5 0 *